Published in Great Britain by L.R. Price Publications Ltd, 2022 27 Old Gloucester Street, London, WC1N 3AX www.lrpricepublications.com

LR Price Publications Ltd Copyright © 2022

Story by S.J. Barker.
S.J. Barker Copyright © 2022

The right of S.J. Barker to be identified as author of this work has been asserted in accordance with sections 77 and 78 of the Copyright, Designs and Patents Act, 1988.

ISBN-: 978-1-916613-12-6

THE POWER OF THE ELEMENTS

THE BEGINNING

by

S. J. Barker

Chapter One

There is no date, no time, no location. Just a world; ravaged by evil, drought, pollution, plague and war. A world that no one wants to remember. Memories give no joy. They are just a reminder of how long people have survived in an unforgiving world.

Surviving with your tribe; finding new places to live, to remain safe from the harsh planet or hidden from the forces of Scorpius, ruler of all. Hoping that they don't find you and take what supplies you have left. No dates, times or locations. Just how long since we were last attacked? How much food do we have left? Are we safe here or do we need to move on? That's how life exists now, no special days. Until today began.

This day was to bring a moment of joy, a moment of renewed life to one family within the tribe. A moment that would bring hope.

Mack and Ava lived within this tribe and like all others, they survived on what little the land had to offer. A dry land, where every drop of water collected was treated as the most valuable commodity; collected from streams that the tribe had gathered around or saved from moisture in the air when the temperature changed between night and day, gathered and scraped from materials hanging from their makeshift homes. Each drop of water used to feed the tribe and what livestock remained.

This was the life of Mack and Ava but they had something more, they had a child. A girl. A teenage girl called Marta. They had hoped that one day this child would wake to a different world. They had hoped that she would not have to live the life that they did. But, at the moment all they hoped for was that she would breathe life.

Marta had been in a long, deep, lifeless sleep. Not death, not a coma but a sleep. A sleep that required no food and water to keep her alive. Just the loving care and attention of Mack and Ava to keep her safe. A sleep she had fallen into some months ago. All had feared the worst. But as time went on and her physical condition never changed, despite the fact that she had not eaten or drank, they realised that this was something different. They believed that one day she would awake once more. That belief and hope were soon to be rewarded.

For Ava, the day began as normal. No date, no time, no location. She went to gather what food was available from the tribe, whilst Mack watched over Marta. He stood over her vigilantly, hoping each day that this would be the one that she awoke. He gazed at his princess, as all girls are to their fathers, and admired her beauty. Her long, dark hair with its tight curls and her rich dark skin, still young. Still not yet showing the age of the tough life they lived. He hoped that soon he would be able to look upon her deep brown eyes.

Ava lined up with others as they were handed what was available, for the day, for each household. There is never any discord between the tribe. They are aware that life is hard enough and always try to be supportive of each other and chat civilly whilst they wait to see what is available to eat. The goats and chickens of the tribe had been able to forage enough to feed themselves and produce milk and eggs. They had been collected and divided amongst each household. Today Ava received a cup of milk, two eggs and some root vegetables grown on the land close to a stream. Not much but compared to some days it was a feast.

She returned home to Mack as he watched over Marta.

"It looks like we have some treats today" said Mack, "and if I know the skills of my beautiful wife, I shall be snoozing with a satisfied belly this afternoon."

Ava smiled. She had always loved that Mack tried to be positive. Despite their wretched times he hadn't given up hope that one day things would be better. She laid down the food, put her arms around him and pressed her cheek into his chest.

"Well if I don't keep that belly happy, I won't have anywhere to lay my head when I sleep."

As they held each other close they heard a sigh. Not loud, not forceful, but a gentle out-take of breath. A slight sound, like that of a breeze passing over the ground. Mack and Ava froze. Not sure if they had really heard something, not daring to move in case the sounds came again. They did come again. A sigh, a yawn, a movement, an awakening!

Mack and Ava rushed to the side of Marta, aware of what was happening. They had waited and desired this moment for many months. This is a moment that parents experience most days. The joy of a much-loved child awakening.

Seeing their eyes open and sharing their love without a word spoken.

"Marta" Ava whispered gently, holding back the excitement and joy that was running through her. "Marta, it's your mother", she whispered gently again, not wanting to startle Marta.

Marta's eyes slowly began to open. Struggling at first, remembering how the eyelids worked. Then, when open, sharply closing again as light became something to get used to once more. Blinking some more until enough practice was done to keep them open. Then confusion in the eyes as Marta struggled to understand why her parents were bent over her with such looks of joy and excitement. Was this not just another day? No date, no time, no location.

Eventually Marta's eyes softened and gently blended with her face, into a smile.

"Hello Mum, Dad" "was it you talking to me. I heard someone telling me it's time to wake up. It didn't sound like you. They said it was important. It was time for it to begin. Although I don't know what it is."

"How do you feel?" Ava asked. "You've been asleep for so long. Tell me, what do you need?"

"I feel" Marta paused for a moment, "I feel strong, I feel full of life and energy. I feel ready."

In a time when no one cares for memories, this is a day to be remembered.

As the days passed Marta began to get used to being amongst the tribe once more. All that saw her were lifted by her presence. A small gift of joy, in a down trodden world. As she walked amongst the tribe, Marta wondered what the voices meant as she slept. What was about to begin and what was her role? She looked at the faces of the tribe; dirty and unkempt. Water was too valuable to use for washing and cleaning. The tribe were currently camped by the side of a stream that gave them just enough water to grow some crops and feed themselves. Certainly not enough to dive in and wallow, surround yourself in cool waters to chill the body and take away the heat from the harsh daytime sun. Surrounding them were steep, jagged cliffs that opened out at each end of the valley, through which the stream flowed. Enough to keep them hidden from the evil forces that may attack but not enough to prevent any if it happened. For now, it had been enough to keep them safe but every member of the tribe knew that it would come soon. That moment when the armies of Scorpius would come and take what little they possessed. They would be no match for them. The armies would be healthy and fit. Enriched from all that they had plundered from around the land.

The tribes' fragile frames, wrapped in whatever materials they could use; anything found, anything that once was used to build their homes but was now too full of holes to use or the hides of animals no longer able to provide food. That was all that they had to protect them. No match when the armies come, and come they would. But when? There were no clues.

No date, no time, no location.

For the moment they waited, they survived, they lived.

Marta wondered what her role would be. Why had she fallen into a deep sleep? Why had she recovered so strong? A voice had spoken to her during her sleep but it was not from her parents. What did the voice that spoke to her, during her sleep, want? What was about to begin and what could she do? She was just a young girl, barely transitioning into a woman. Surely there was nothing she could do.

"It is time Marta" said a voice. Marta startled and looked for where the voice was coming from.

"It is time to learn". As much as Marta looked, there was no one there, no one with her. Although, it was as clear as if someone standing next to her had just spoken. It was evident that she was the only one that could hear the voice. It wasn't a voice that scared her. It was gentle enough to make her feel at ease. A young voice, like her own.

"Learn what? Who are you? Why can I hear you but not see you?" Marta asked.

"In time you will know but first you must learn. Learn what you are capable of. Learn what you must achieve. Learn what is to be your future."

"Ok, ok, I get you" Marta replied. "Let me find some place to be alone and we can talk. Standing in the middle of the tribe talking to myself is hardly reassuring to people watching me."

Marta made her way to the edge of the tribe and up the steep inclines at the base of the cliffs, searching for a place that no one could see her and could most certainly not hear her.

"Ok, I'm in the clear now. What do you want to teach me?"

"Do you feel the earth beneath your feet?" said the voice.

"Of course, it's always there, not just beneath, but in between and in my nails. Nothing new there for a barefoot person. Not exactly something I needed to learn" Marta quipped.

"You can feel what you can see. But can you feel what you can't?" the voice replied.

"What? If you're going to be in my head, you're going to need to be a bit clearer with the lesson plan, I think."

"Feel the earth beyond what you see. Feel beneath that."

"Ok, if you say so" Marta replied, as she crouched down and started to scrape away at the ground beneath her.

"Not with your hands but with your mind Marta."

"Right, you want me to feel the earth with my mind? Are you crazy! How am I going to do that? Or is this just some strange thing that I'm telling myself?" Marta exclaimed. She then checked herself and her surroundings, realising that she had become loud and didn't wish to draw any attention.

"I think I might need some clearer instructions here, as it's all sounding a bit weird."

"Stand still, close your eyes. First feel the earth that is around your feet. Feel the physical, surface upon surface. Allow that sensation to move through your body."

Marta did as she was told.

"Do you feel the earth, do you feel the sensation moving into your body?"

"I do."

"Now feel what is below."

Marta paused for a moment and opened her eyes. Again, doubting the sanity of what the voice was telling her. Then closed them once more and began to concentrate.

She could feel the earth that touched her feet, hot and dry. She allowed that sensation to pass through her body. It was uncomfortable, as all of her body could now sense the dusty crust of the earth immediately beneath her.

"It's hot" she said.

"Then cool yourself," replied the voice, "feel the earth beneath the surface. Feel the earth that has not been scorched by the sun."

Marta concentrated. She let her mind drift through her body and down into ground beneath her feet. The further she let her mind travel, the cooler she became as she felt the earth deeper below the surface, further from the sun. Earth that contained moisture, earth that contained the beginnings of life.

"How wonderful. I can sense it all."

"Now physically feel it, bring the earth to you. Surround yourself with it" the voice said.

As she concentrated harder, the soil beneath her feet began to shift slightly. Not much, no more than if a breeze had dusted her feet with it. She concentrated harder. It felt like her own energy was reaching out of her body and digging into the soil like roots of a tree; feeding on the life below her. The more the roots expanded, the more the earth moved as it became displaced. What was a slight breeze of a movement was becoming stronger beneath her. A shake and a push as the earth began to rise.

"Gently" the voice cautioned. But by this point Marta was emotionally immersed in what she was feeling. As the excitement and joy she was feeling increased, so did the movement of the earth beneath her.

"Careful" the voice cautioned once more.

"This feels so good! So alive!" Screamed Marta.

As the surge of excitement raced through Marta the earth began to move more fervently, climbing higher and higher up.

"You need more control" urged the voice.

"What do you mean I am... aaargh!" She screamed as she realised that she was now completely surrounded by the earth. It was all over her and beginning to get in her face and hair. Marta realised that she was burying herself in a mound of earth.

"Stop this, stop this at once" she screamed.

Her concentration was broken and so was her connection with the earth. In an instant the earth stopped moving. Marta realised that she was covered and began do dig herself out of the mound that she had created.

"Great, just great. I really needed a lesson in how to make myself even dirtier." In that moment Marta realised she could hear laughter. It was the voice.

"Are you laughing at me?"

"Indeed. I wouldn't worry. It happens every time."

"Excellent, that makes me feel slightly less stupid. Wait! Hang on, does that mean there are others, you know, like me?"

"Similar but different. Close but far. All in time Marta" the voice replied. "But that is enough for today, you need to rest and we shall begin again tomorrow."

"Wonderful. Hopefully you won't find me so amusing tomorrow."

"You do amuse me a lot" replied the voice.

"How come?"

"Well you don't actually need to speak out loud to talk to me. I can read your mind. But it is funny to see you talking to no one. I shall leave you now to rest and we shall begin again on the new day."

"Great, not only do I have a voice in my head but they think they are funny. Furthermore, why am I still talking out loud when they're not here anymore?"

With that, Marta returned home to get some rest. Quite clearly there was a lot more to learn.

Over the passing days Marta did learn a lot indeed. She learned how to control the earth; how to command it to her will. All under the guidance of the voice in her head. As she learned more, she put it to good use. She realised that by bringing earth from deep down, that had not been scorched from the sun, she could make the lands that the tribe inhabited, more fertile. So, under the cover of night she would practice her skills, gently and quietly so as to not wake anyone. When the tribe awoke each morning, they would find their surroundings less barren and more hospitable. She would flatten areas to make them easier to work and easier to plant more crops. Marta was subtle in her changes, not wishing to arouse suspicion. She made it seem that the tribe had become blessed. That their lands had become enriched naturally. That their small piece of this cruel world had come to life and in turn was giving them renewed life too.

She continued her learning. She continued to use what she learned. As the days continued, turning into weeks and into months, she continued to thrive, as did all that surrounded her.

One day, Marta sat high up on the cliffs watching over her tribe. What had once been a harsh unforgiving landscape, was now an oasis. The once wretched faces of the people were now healthier. Still dark in complexion from the endless sun but less worn and battered. Even a little cleaner. The bodies a little stronger. No longer the hunched forms of endless toil. Some of this came from their bodies getting stronger and some from a renewed sense of hope. A feeling of each day may get better, each day might be worth living and each day it was worth waking to.

The tribe was becoming stronger, not just in body but in mind and also in their bonds between each other.

As Marta sat, the voice spoke to her once more.

 "You have done well. Your tribe has renewed life. They will thrive."

"Thank you" replied Marta.

"I am only a guide. This is all your doing."

"I feel great. I feel strong and healthy like everyone else. But this isn't all of it. I wasn't given this skill just for this, was I?"

"You are connected to the earth. Your strength comes from it now. But no, this is not your purpose. This is where it will begin. Your skills will be needed in different ways, some will be easy and some will be hard. Some days you will question whether you want your skills; whether their use is right, correct, and moral. You will not only need your strength of body but also that of your mind, in order to make the right choices. These will not always be the best for you but they will be the choices you have to make."

"I had a feeling there would be a catch" Marta responded. "You said this is where it would begin. Has it not begun yet, is this, all this that I have created, that we have created, is it not the beginning. If not, then what is? Please tell. Please, please tell me, I need to know. Teach me! Show me!"

"You have learned a lot Marta. But so far you have used your skill for life, for enrichment. And this has brought with it joy and happiness. You have learned all this and you have experienced, sensed and felt all this. But for it to begin, there must be a balance. You must experience the other side to what your skills can bring, feel and sense what they are."

Marta sat motionless, realising the gravity of what had been said. Hoping that the words of the voice were not what she believed them to be.

"You mean loss, sadness, pain and all the other bad things that I can think of right now. Don't you. Don't you?"

For a moment there was silence, before the voice spoke again.

"I do, that is the balance to your skills. You must experience them all."

"Then I don't want them. Take them back. Leave me alone!"

"I did not give you your skills. They were born to you, just as mine were, just as the others were" the voice replied.

"And the others, they have this balance too?"

"When it begins, they shall have balance also."

Marta sat motionless once more, as she allowed the gravity of what had just been said sink in. Then she gave a twitch, a shake and a long exasperated sigh.

"Boy, you really know how to bring a girl down don't you? Oh no, you couldn't let this just be it." Marta paused for a moment and then began to smile. "Do you even exist, or is there chance I'm just crazy and I could just ignore you?"

"I exist and in time you shall know me" came the voice.

"Well, when and if I ever get to know you, there's going to be an awfully uncomfortable moment when I may want to shake you."

"In time you will know the answer to that and it will be obvious."

"Brilliant, I love the way that you're always so clear."

"You mock me."

"Yes, I do my friend. I think I've earned that. Now, let's get back to the tribe. I get the feeling I should enjoy this whilst I can."

As she wandered back down to the tribe and through the people, she revelled in seeing the happiness that the current situation brought. How long would this happiness last though? If the voice were to be believed, then there would yet be harder times to come and maybe soon. However, there was nothing she could do. No one was aware that it is her that had created their fortuitous situation. They are happy to be blessed at this moment and did not question how or why this had happened.

Marta returned to her home. As she arrived, she could see her parents standing outside. They too were observing the inhabitants of the tribe. They too were enjoying the changes that they were witnessing.

"Ah, here comes our baby. How are you my princess?" Mack cried out on seeing Marta.

"Dad, you're so embarrassing. I'm not a baby anymore or a princess."

"You will always be my princess and baby. Even when you're grown up and have kids of your own. That's my right as your father. To call you what I like and to embarrass you." Mack laughed as he enjoyed amusing himself.

"I don't suppose you're going to stop him are you Mother?" Marta asked.

"Of course not, he wouldn't be the man I love if he wasn't a bit daft."

Marta's face wrinkled slightly at the realisation that her parents could be a bit silly and embarrassing at times but this was how they were and secretly she loved them for it.

"There is so much to be grateful for" Mack interjected "the land has become fertile and we can eat well. Also, my beautiful daughter has returned to us. We have been twice blessed. I can't think of anything that should stop me from being a bit daft right now. This is most definitely a time to be happy. To enjoy life, to sing a little, to dance a little. In fact, I think we need to have a party to celebrate. Better yet, a festival. The whole tribe!" Mack exclaimed. "What do you think?"

"Sounds wonderful!" Ava said

"Dad, I think you may have had a good idea. Steady on!" Marta cheekily added.

"Right that's it then. I'm off to speak to others in the tribe. It's time we enjoyed ourselves" and with that Mack strode off with purpose. Intent on sharing his idea with all that would listen.

A festival! Why not indeed, thought Marta. Let the good times happen, enjoy it while we can. Although the voice has told her that she would have to experience the bad, she might as well enjoy the good. Anyway, who knows when bad things might happen? Maybe tomorrow, maybe next week or month or year. There was no clear message as to when Marta was to experience anything bad. So why worry, it may never come.

There is no date, no time, no location.

Chapter Two

Scorpius

A palace like no other place in the world. Surrounded by its opulent kingdom. No one here is starving. No one here is unhealthy. No one here wonders how they will survive. Food is plentiful. Lavish accommodation and high standards of living are the standard. Strength and wellbeing positively gush from its inhabitants. This is a kingdom with all the amenities of a modern world. A life that has not seen the suffering that others beyond this kingdom endure. This is a life supplied by the suffering of others beyond their realm. Living here is a choice. A choice to be well looked after. A choice not to care about the troubles outside of this kingdom. A choice to be part of the kingdom that rules over all. In doing so, you choose to be loyal to one. The one that rules. If you live here, you choose to be loyal and serve. Serve the almighty leader. The all-powerful leader. Scorpius.

There is no question of morals here. For if you are here, you believe that what you are doing is right. If you questioned that, the fear would soon correct you. No one would dare question that Scorpius, the almighty ruler, was in any way wrong and the very rare few that did, were never seen again.

The kingdom is power, strength and greatness. Wealth, beauty and opulence. A dream of a world to live in, created by the great mind of Scorpius. A place safe from the cruel and harsh surroundings of the outside world. A place made safe by Scorpius. A place to be well fed and looked after, by the generous Scorpius.

In this kingdom, Scorpius was all and everything. The mighty leader, the mighty warrior, the magnificence that must be revered; that must be followed without question. The almighty that deserved the worship of all those that lived in the kingdom. Always and forever.

As Scorpius was the centre of all in the kingdom, so was his palace. High it rose, in the middle so that Scorpius could witness all and rule everything. The walls of the palace bled precious metals and jewels gathered from all corners of the world. Tall and imposing, impressive to all that witnessed it. A palace fit for a king, a lord, a deity. Resplendent in its glorious presence above all the world, for all to see and be seen.

As you enter the palace through its high and wide heavy gilded doors, into the long and imposing corridors; you will see jewels and pictures beyond compare. Anything of value, from all corners of the world, has been taken and has made its way to this point to be on display. Let there be no mistake, this palace displays the ultimate power that it houses. This palace is undeniably the palace of Scorpius.

In its centre is the throne room, where Scorpius controls all on a daily basis. This is where decisions are of life and death. They centre on one man, one throne, one ultimate ruler. This day was to begin like all others, where all that served Scorpius firsthand, gathered in the throne room to await their almighty ruler's presence. They were there to hear his orders and to carry out his every request or demand. Failure was most definitely not an option. Although they gave their all to adhere to their leader's demands willingly, there was always fear. For failure would be met with the harshest of punishments. But faithfully and loyally they gather and await his arrival. Wondering what his commands would be. Some hoping that today would be their day to be called upon to serve. Some hoping that they would not, fearing that they might fail and face retribution. All wait for his arrival and that of his constant companion, his daughter Lyra.

Today the wait was not long. Scorpius entered from behind the throne, which could be seen on a higher level atop a wide set of stairs. He was dressed, as most were used to seeing him, all in black with gold adornments breaking the lines of his clothing. He was tall and fit. His skin smooth and tanned. His face and head hairless, emphasising his deep piercing eyes and his sharp jawline and cheeks. This was a man who appeared flawless at all times. No weakness but all power.

Beside him stood his daughter Lyra. Her beauty was famed throughout all the world and to see her was to bathe in her magnificence. She was also tall. Her curves flowed around her body with perfect proportion. Her face was perfect in every way. A beauty beyond compare, framed within her dark, lustrous, flowing hair. Her eyes are deep and dark but have a fire within that can draw in any person. Although, as the stories told, being drawn in by Lyra was very dangerous indeed. Anyone enamoured by the undeniable beauty of Lyra could find themselves in danger. For Lyra had powers beyond all men and women. Dark powers that could destroy all. Resisting the attraction would be almost impossible but all must try to avoid this temptress' charms.

As Scorpius and Lyra entered, everyone bowed in homage to their presence. No one would dare to offend by failing to do so. No one would dare to catch the unnecessary attention of Scorpius and Lyra. Scorpius came to his throne, he gently and quietly sat, adjusting himself for comfort. He took his time, for when you are the most powerful, you can take as long as you desire. Lyra stood slightly behind and to the side of the throne. Ready and on hand if needed. Behind her stood the servants, who wait hand and foot upon the rulers; as well as the chief politicians who administer their master's will. Finally, when Scorpius feels that all who are gathered have subjugated themselves enough, he began to speak.

He spoke in a clear, precise and educated voice.

"Welcome all, shall we get down to business?" He gazed around the room, calculating where best to start, in order to carry out the day's meeting in a timely and efficient manner. He selected the man in charge of agriculture.

"I believe our food supplies a good, are they not? I assume there has been no problems in acquiring and replenishing all that we need?"

A man boldly stepped forward.

"Indeed, my Lord, we have plenty of provisions. Although, I believe we will need to find some tribes that we can acquire more from. The ones that we have plundered recently have had very little."

"These tribes, people were alive, were they not?" Scorpius responded.

"Yes, my Lord."

"Then they must have supplies. Do make sure that we receive all that they have. If they choose not to give generously to their ruler, remind them of how generous they need to be. We certainly don't wish them to think that ruling over all is easy and that we do not need sustenance in order to do so. Make sure these people understand!"

"Yes, my Lord."

"You!" Scorpius pointed at a large man wearing uniform and armour. He stepped forward and saluted Scorpius. "As commander of my armies, make sure this is carried out without mercy, do you understand?"

"Yes, my Lord" the commander responded.

"Do we also have scouting parties out looking for new places to acquire supplies?"

"We do my Lord."

"And what news from these scouts?"

"Positive news, we have discovered a tribe that is living a comfortable existence. Their land seems to have become enriched and they appear to have an abundance of supplies. We have been keeping watch over them from a distance. Waiting for the right moment to attack."

There is a moment of silence. All looked to Scorpius who seemed to have become very agitated all of a sudden.

"Enriched land, you say. Would you say that this land has been this way for a while?"

"No my Lord, the area surrounding this particular tribe is very barren and mountainous but they appear to have been able to cultivate the land that they live on."

"Remarkable!" Shouted Scorpius. "Sounds like something of a miracle. An oasis in a desert. You wouldn't say that this was in anyway, suspicious? Or that I probably should have known about this sooner?" Scorpius asked sarcastically.

The commander stumbled for words and so Scorpius continued.

"No, you didn't. Of course not. Why would you? You don't do your own thinking, that's why you need me." Scorpius stood and addressed the room. "We have a tribe that has magically taken a barren piece of land and brought it to life. They are living the good life. It's a miracle! So what does this tribe do? Do they give thanks to the mighty Scorpius and inform him of their fortunes. No. They hide away and keep everything for themselves. Why? Because we let them! We stayed at a distance and watched." Scorpius paused for a moment and then looked at the commander. "It's not your fault. Why should I be surprised or angered? You're a soldier, you need orders. I should try harder to not be so disappointed." He paused for a moment and turned to his daughter. "Don't you agree Lyra?"

Lyra had been waiting with mischievous anticipation. She moved from behind Scorpius' chair and began to interact with her father.

"Yes Daddy, poor soldier, he's not to know."

"Indeed Lyra, do you think Daddy should show some sympathy for him? Do you think daddy should be wise and teach him the error of his ways?"

"Yes Daddy, don't be cruel to the poor soldier. He's just a little stupid. Let's be kind. Let me show him some love."

"This must be your lucky day commander. Despite your stupidity and incompetence, my beautiful daughter is feeling generous and thoughtful. Do you not agree commander?"

"Yes, my Lord." Responded the commander. Despite his positive reply there was a hesitancy in his voice, for he was doubtful that he was about to be forgiven without consequences. No one ever was.

"Well, my dearest daughter, I shall let you proceed. Show us all how merciful we can be, despite of the failure that has occurred."

"Yes Daddy." Lyra moved forward, towards all that had gathered whilst Scorpius sat down again upon his throne.

Lyra slowly descended the stairs toward the commander. As with all things that she did, she moved with effortless grace and poise. All the time her eyes were fixed upon the commander, whilst he began to look increasingly nervous.

"Don't be afraid solder" she said. "Daddy can be tough. He doesn't understand that sometimes people need to be treated differently. Sometimes people need love and understanding. Sometimes they need a gentle kiss and a song. That gets better results, sometimes."

Lyra stared intently into the commander's eyes. She gently caressed the side of his face. All the while the commander was looking more nervous as he wondered what was about to happen. Lyra then kissed the palm of her hand and blew the kiss into the face of the commander. As she did, a look of joy began to spread across his face. The gentle breeze of the kiss caressed his face and began to bring on a euphoria of happiness. In a moment, the commander was experiencing nothing but joy. He had been intoxicated by Lyra.

"You see Daddy, look how happy he is. No need to be so mean."

"I do indeed my beautiful daughter, teach us some more." Scorpius responded.

"Now I think my lovely soldier needs a song." Lyra continued. By this point the commander was completely lost in a high of joy. He was swaying and beginning to chuckle to himself like a child. Lyra began to sing.

"Soldier, soldier, come to me. Soldier, soldier, let me see. Listen to my voice hear me sing. Then feel what my voice will bring. Then listen to it for a thousand years. Because then you can feel the tears."

As Lyra repeated herself over and over, the tension in the room increased as all gathered realised that she was creating a powerful enchantment over the commander and that something bad was about to happen.

Lyra continued with her song. Her manner was seductive and she continued to gently caress the commander like a lover would.

By this point the commander was completely enraptured by the seduction of Lyra. The euphoria within him built higher and higher. His face was lit up like a child that can no longer contain himself. His laughter increased out of control. Faster and faster, louder and louder he laughed until he found himself struggling to breathe enough air, to continue the laughter. He began to gasp for air but still continued to laugh. Then he realised what was happening to him and grabbed at the side of his head; trying to stop the sound of Lyra's voice from penetrating through his ears into his mind. The laughter changed into gasps and screams of panic; as the song began to cause pain, burning into his brain. Relentlessly it continued to cause hurt and anguish. More pain, endlessly attacking him. The commander fell to the floor. The laughter was now completely replaced by screams of pain and desire for mercy.

Lyra stopped singing and stood over the commander. He continued to scream. As it was said in the song, he would hear the voice for a thousand years. Lyra smiled mischievously and looked around the room at all who had witnessed what had just happened. Almost all tried to show no emotion. They did not wish to offend Lyra, in her moment of triumph. She had quite clearly enjoyed herself and no one wished her to gain further pleasure at their expense.

"I don't think he likes my song Daddy." Lyra turned to her father and looked to him like a child that had been upset by her innocent actions.

"Never mind my dear, some people don't have an ear for music. I hope this hasn't upset you too much."

"A little bit Daddy but I will get over it." Lyra then returned up the stairs to be by the side of her father. Scorpius stood, once more, to address all that were gathered. He realised that the screaming commander needed to be removed and gesticulated for him to be taken from the room, which was carried out at speed.

"Who is second in command?"

Another soldier reluctantly stepped forward.

"Congratulations on your promotion." As Scorpius began to clap, so did all that were gathered and the soldier bowed towards his leader in a show of gratitude.

Scorpius stopped clapping and all the other applause quickly died out, as all waited for their leader to begin speaking once more.

"Foolishness will not be tolerated. If you have any doubts about what is the correct course of action, then I suggest you seek advice. That advice should always be to inform me immediately. Because my mind is quicker than yours. My mind is informed and knowledgeable. My mind will make the correct decision for all those in this world. If you doubt that, you may run away. But be assured that I will always find you and I will always correct you. Do I make myself clear?"

"Yes, my Lord" responded all.

"Good." Scorpius paused for a moment, as he gathered his thoughts.

"We have here a situation where a tribe has riches. Rather than share those riches, they have decided to keep it a secret. Why have they done that? What are they hiding from us? Do they not wish to share this wondrous bounty will their generous leader and give thanks for his magnanimous guidance in keeping them safe during these harsh and unforgiving times?" Scorpius rose once more to speak to all assembled. "No. Instead they choose to be selfish, to ignore the needs of others for the purpose of their own gain, for their own gratification. They must be evil and ruthless, to disregard all others but themselves. They do not understand that we here have the never-ending toil of ruling over everyone and that toil needs to be fed and nourished in order to continue such a task. If we were to wither and die, so would the rest of the world, without our leadership and knowledge to help them to survive. They do not understand, they do not see the sacrifice that we make for them. So, they need to be educated. Not just them but all others like them, who think this is how the world works. They must learn how to behave and how to yield to their benevolent ruler. If not, we will have anarchy and the selfish will have won, leading to the demise of all. There will be others like this, others that choose to be selfish. So, if we leave this tribe untouched then all the other selfish inhabitants of the world will thrive. Therefore, we must send a message to all that this will not be tolerated. So that all can learn and be educated from this tribe's mistakes. We must seek out this tribe and others that may also be thriving without sharing their good fortunes. We must educate them in the ways of the world. We must show them that their selfishness and disobedience comes with terrifying consequences, so that all others will know that we do not allow this!"

All that were gathered begin to holler and cheer. Scorpius took a moment to enjoy the response to his triumphant speech and then silenced the crowd with a gesture from his hand. He composed himself and began again.

"Too kind, I truly am not worthy of your admiration." He stated, with false modesty. "Commander, send out the troops to this tribe. Also, seek out others like them and make our message clear. Take all that they have, for they have very likely already gorged themselves enough and need to learn that this is not acceptable. Then we shall be merciful, for it would be cruel to leave them with no provisions to survive. They would surely suffer a slow and painful death in this cruel world. So we shall be merciful by making their death quick and painless. All will be educated when they see how kind we have been to them. Do I make myself clear, commander?"

"Yes, my Lord."

"Then make it so. There is no time to waste. Leave us now. We all have a lot to do."

Everyone began to leave. A few approached Scorpius trying to engage him in other business but were waved away until all that remained were Scorpius, Lyra and their personal protection guards; who stayed in the shadows in order not to intrude upon their leaders. Lyra began to speak.

"Are you fearful Daddy?"

"Why would I be fearful Lyra?"

"Because you believe that there is more to this than just chance. That there is something more to this tribe. When I was younger and I used to hear the voice that taught me about my powers, it used to talk about balance. It used to tell me that there would be others like me, with powers. That they would experience good and bad like me. That is what the voice told me and I told you. Do you fear this Daddy? Do you worry that they might bring our world to an end?"

"I fear nothing Lyra. In order for things to come to an end, there has to be a beginning. I will make sure that it does not happen, by making sure it no longer exists. You were young when you heard the voice. It was nothing more than a childhood delusion that ended when your mother died. Everything will be dealt with, whether it be just chance, a prophecy or just a childhood fantasy. Worry not child, I will take care of it all."

"Yes Daddy"

"Now let us go check on the troops, they have a lot to do. We must stop any chance of a mini rebellion before it begins and restore order."

Chapter Three

A Festival

There is no date, no time, no location but today was to be different, today was to be remembered. Today was the festival in Marta's tribe. Today they would give thanks for their recent good fortune. Although no one knew how it had happened, with the exception of Marta herself, they certainly wanted to give thanks and enjoy all the fine harvests that they were having. Marta's father Mack had suggested a celebration with a festival and all had quickly agreed. At last joy and happiness were to rule over their lives for once and they certainly didn't want it to end.

Marta woke to the bustling of the tribe. Makeshift decorations adorning every available space. People preparing food, in readiness for a banquet. Old instruments that have not seen the light of day for a very long time, were dusted off. Their players practiced how to make music once more; shakily at first, with a fair few off-key notes. Eventually flowing into some recognisable tunes. The tribe was alive once more with an energy that had disappeared a long time ago. Marta looked around and was filled with excitement and joy. She had done this. Her ever developing powers had created this. As she walked amongst the tribe she revelled in the positive emotions. The tribe had always been united. Never split or divided by disagreements or arguments. Never split by ethnicity or beliefs. This was one unit, one tribe, one community, one big family.

Marta passed through everyone and found somewhere to be alone.

"Thank you for all this." Marta said to the voice.

"I have not done this" replied the voice, "I have just guided you, the power is yours. Without you none of this was possible."

"I see. I need to ask you so much. Who are you? Will I ever actually meet you or are you just some crazy thought in my head? You can see my concerns." Marta asked.

"All will become clear over time. For now, enjoy yourself and do not question what you think or feel. When the time comes it will be important for you not to delay but to respond instantly."

"Boy, you certainly like to make things murky." Marta laughed at the sarcastic criticism that she had placed upon the voice.

"You may not understand at the moment but you will and soon. I promise."

"Cool, I think. Anyway, let's go and enjoy ourselves. I heard someone has been making some hooch. I can't wait to try that."

"Aren't you a bit young for that?" Responded the voice.

"Wow, you are such a nerd. I already have parents, I don't need a lesson from you too! Can I not just have some fun?"

"Sorry, proceed with the festivities."

"That's another thing, even your language is nerdy." Marta laughed again at her own sarcasm. "Come on, let's go."

She returned again to join the mass of the tribe. They were in full swing. In the middle was her father, Mack, who is dancing wildly and getting the assembled crowd going. Whilst Marta may pretend that she is embarrassed by it, she was actually overjoyed; just like her mother who was also witness to her husband's behaviour and was enjoying every moment of it. Love often makes you proud of some of the strangest moments and to Ava, this was one of those times. A moment to be treasured and, more importantly, to be remembered. As Marta watched the proceedings she could hear a voice calling her. She turned and there in front of her was an old friend, Rags.

Rags was a long-time friend that she had known since she was very young. He was of similar age and so they had often spent time together, growing up.

Rags was not his real name. It was however, what everyone called him. No matter how much his parents had tried to keep him vaguely presentable with freshly made clothes and an occasional wash, it would not be long before his adventurous spirit would have reduced his latest set of clothes to rags. Hence the name. In fact he had been known by that name for so long, very few could remember his actual name, given at birth.

Rags rushed to greet Marta, filled with excitement at seeing his long-time friend. With Marta keeping herself separate from most within the tribe, whilst she developed her powers, she had not seen much of her friend. She too was overjoyed. Rags was always good fun. On a day, like today, his presence was an added bonus on top of the festivities. However, she suddenly realised that there were some more emotions added on to her usual pleasure at seeing Rags.

He had changed. Rags had always been an energetic and adventurous type and because of this his frame had always been thin and scrawny. There had never been enough food to feed his way of living and as such he had always had the appearance of someone that could be blown over at the slightest of breezes. But things were different now. Food was plentiful, so Rags had started to fill out and develop into a fully-grown man. No longer was Marta looking at a weak looking boy. Now Rags was a muscular young adult. His skin was no longer ravaged from the elements but had a golden tan, highlighting his deep green eyes and his sun-bleached hair. His clothing was still sparse and unkempt but this now revealed more of his outstanding structure. The new emotions that Marta was feeling at seeing Rags were not just excitement at seeing her friend but also that of attraction. Rags threw, his now muscular, arms around Marta. As much as he had grown up so had Marta and she enjoyed his embrace. Not only was it warm and secure within his arms, he also smelled nice, which is not something that she had experienced before within his company. With the scarcity of water previously, the smell of dirt and hard toil had become commonplace amongst the tribe. So, to be swept up into the arms of someone who smelled fresh and of the newly revived land, was somewhat enjoyable. Marta wallowed in this moment, maybe for a bit too long, as she let herself slip into a dream state and let out a long sigh as she relished the experience. Rags realised that the situation was becoming slightly awkward and eased himself apart so he could look at her face.

"You ok?" He asked.

"Yes, yes, all good." Marta quickly responded, trying to cover her embarrassment at the slightly uncomfortable exchange. "So pleased to see you." She paused for a moment. "So much has changed, it just caught me out for a moment." She smiled up at him innocently. Whilst on one hand she hoped he would accept her excuse, she also wished he wouldn't and also felt a change in the chemistry between them.

"I understand. Things have changed so much. But it's all good. I thought when you fell into the deep sleep that things couldn't be much worse. I thought I had lost you for good. But then you woke up and things changed. Look how healthy everyone is. Look at the land it's so beautiful." He hesitated for a moment, checking whether he should proceed. "It's beautiful, just like you." He blushed slightly at his attempt at being romantic and laughed awkwardly. Marta's smile broadened at what she has just heard. She wondered how she should respond to his flattery, as it has come out of the blue from someone she has known for so long. Their previous exchanges had usually involved playing in the dirt of their barren surroundings, there were no such feelings of romance before.

"Well thank you Rags. I can't recall you being so pleasant to me before. Are you sure that you haven't found some bug in the dirt that you are going to try and make me eat? That's how it's been for most of our lives." She laughed at the memory and many more like that from their past. Rags laughed too. They were different times, a lot more harsh but also a lot more innocent than what was unfolding right now.

"No bugs this time. But maybe in the future if you upset me." He smiled at his cheeky quip. Marta was drawn into his charms, as though she was witnessing them for the first time. He was talking about happy times still to come. How wonderful that at last someone could talk about future happiness, the thought of this had been so alien in recent times. Marta is snapped from her daydream state when Rags talked again.

"Come on, let's join the fun."

He took her by the hand and pulled her into the midst of all the fun. Despite the physical changes, Rags had not lost any enthusiasm for life. As they passed through the crowds, he grabbed a tankard of the, much anticipated, hooch and swigged down a large gulp or two before he handed it to Marta and she did the same. They reached where Marta's parents have been enjoying themselves and began to join in the revelries. Ava noticed that the two youngsters had joined them and acknowledged their presence. She too had noticed the development of Rags and gave Marta a knowing look, before she grabbed Mack and guided him away from the young couple. She knew that, as much as she loved Mack's silliness, now was not the time to have him near the pair. Moreover, perhaps today was not the time to realise that his young princess was growing up.

Marta and Rags begin to move to the music. As much as they are aware of dancing, it was not something that they have had much chance to do previously and to begin with their movements were a bit wild and erratic. As time passed and the hooch began to kick in, they become more relaxed and the dancing began to flow with more ease. What also began to flow more, was the attraction between them and as the dancing increased, so did the connection and closeness between the pair. Eventually they no longer felt awkward about the attraction and their dancing became entwined. Marta became intoxicated, not only by the hooch, but also with the close proximity of Rags. As he surrounded her, with his arms, she was completely overjoyed. There was definitely no better place to be right now, safe and secure within his strong arms. She placed her head on his muscular chest and allowed herself to indulge in this moment. He caressed the back of her neck and ran his hands through her hair. She was enraptured and hoped the moment will never end. Eventually, she pulled back slightly from him and looked up at him to talk.

"Well who knew that I was going to feel like this with you?" She said.

"I never knew but I always hoped." Responded Rags. Marta looked surprised at this statement. Rags continued.

"I've always liked you. Obviously, when we were much younger it was a childhood friend thing. But as we got older it turned into something more. You were always the coolest, so eventually it turned into a crush."

"Wow, that's a surprise. I never saw it. Me, the coolest, really?" As she said this she laughed, which then developed into something else, a kind of a snort brought on by the unexpected situation.

"Ok, so that was embarrassing. Just goes to show that I'm not cool at all. Are you sure that this is what you like?"

"I've never been so sure of anything Marta. Things are becoming so much better, with all the food and the life we have now. There's just one thing left to make it perfect and that's you."

Marta tried to speak but was lost for words. She just looked up at Rags and smiled. Could this moment be any more perfect she wondered. Then Rags leaned down and gently kissed her on the lips. So soft and gentle. A little hesitant at first as they have had no experience of doing this before. Then again, more confident this time in what they were doing and certain that they wouldn't be rejected. As they finished Marta buried herself deep within his arms and rested her head against his chest. She hoped that this moment would last for ever. For so long Marta and all around her had dreamt of a different life, a life. Away from the daily toil of survival. At last they could make memories and look to a more exciting future and all this could be found within the arms of Rags.

As they slowly moved to the music, Rags held Marta tight. He had waited so long for this and didn't want to let her go. Marta was happy with this too. Then, in the distance, a high-pitched sound could be heard. Getting closer and louder within a split of a second. And then it hit! A blow shook Rags that then reverberated into Marta. Then more and more rained down on everyone. Arrows! The armies of Scorpius had arrived!

Chapter Four

The Attack

Arrows rained down upon Marta's tribe. The level of fear and panic instantly reached an unprecedented high, as all began to scatter and seek safety. They had been attacked by the armies of Scorpius before but not usually like this. Previously, when the troops had arrived there was never much resistance and so instant show of force was not usual. Normally they would come, take all the food and supplies then leave. There would be a show of force, in order to show what might happen but generally it was no more than show as everybody usually complied. This was a whole new action by the army. Arrows flew everywhere without discrimination, in order to inflict as much instant damage as possible. Marta looked up at Rags, who had his arms around her from the dancing but was now creating a protective shield.

"We need to move Rags, let's get out of here and find somewhere safe."

Rags did nothing.

"We need to move Rags!" She bellowed at him once more, making herself heard over the ever increasing commotion.

Again, Rags did nothing. She looked up at him and realised the reason for his motionless demeanour. She stared long into his eyes and over his face, then the cold realisation hit her. Rags was not moving because he was not able too. The very first arrow that had flown into their gathering had struck Rags. It had hit him in the back and that was the reverberation that Marta had first felt. He was standing purely because he was balanced against Marta. As she stepped back from Rags to try to gain his attention, he began to slide down Marta and fell to the floor. Marta tried to keep him upright in a defiant gesture against what had happened but his size overcame her. He was shot, he was bleeding and he was beginning to die.

"No! No! Not now, this can't happen now." She looked around, desperately trying to find help but everyone was scattering as she screamed unheard beside her stricken man. She mustered the strength to slowly start moving his body whilst there was still life in him. She needed to get him to safety before any more injury befell him. She managed to pull him to a table and then covered him with it. At least he would be safe from the rainfall of arrows showering down upon the tribe. Many stories had been told of the tactics of Scorpius' troops. The shower of arrows was only the first stage. Far worse was yet to come. The armies had amassed all the weapons from around the world and if the need arose, they would use more fearsome and deadly artillery at each stage. To begin they will use the most basic of arms that could easily be replenished. If they could defeat an enemy, without resorting to their advanced weapons, so much the better. First the arrows, then the guns and next the armoured vehicles. In this new world there were no gunpowder factories, so not to wasting a bullet on someone regarded as worthless by the rulers, was the usual. But all were available and ready to be used. If all failed, they could bring the armoured vehicles, no longer running on petrol but now powered with fossil fuel, mined by the slaves of the ruler. These vehicles bellowed through any terrain. Their appearance alone struck fear into all that witnessed them. Large and imposing, heavily armoured in metal, blowing out smoke and steam, in order to create propulsion. Many soldiers sat upon these vehicles, ready to use the most fearsome of weapons accrued from around the world. Destruction was inevitable when all these weapons were used and destruction was quite clearly the plan today.

Marta remained hidden, whilst the deluge of arrows rained down. Rags remained within her arms, as the life slowly continued to seep out of him. Marta's rage began to swell more and more with each arrow strike. Many arrows hit nothing but some struck members of the tribe. Each strike pounded into Marta's heart and inflamed her emotions. She could not see her parents. Each moment that they were out of sight, not knowing whether they were safe, was moment too long. She needed to do something before they were all wiped out. This was clearly not a foray into the tribe for supplies. This was an annihilation. She needed to do something or everyone would be dead. There was nothing to debate.

Marta carefully laid Rags down onto the ground. She tenderly looked at him, aware that this could be the last time. As the emotions of the moment gripped her, she placed her hands on the ground to steady herself. As she did this, she could feel the movement of the soil beneath her. She could feel the displacement of the earth from the advancing armies hundreds of metres away. She could feel it all. She could feel the power of it all! As her emotions became stronger, so did her connection with the earth. It fuelled her, strengthened her, made her powerful! She knew at once what she could do. No one could stop her! Not even an army!

Marta moved from beneath the table and stood with her feet placed firmly on the ground. As she witnessed the armies and their weapons travelling ever closer, she gathered herself and concentrated on the task at hand. She knew she had to let her reservations go, act on instinct and let her power come full force.

Another shower of arrows came raining towards her. She raised her arms and as she did so the soil flew up from the ground and knocked the arrows from their flight. Another set of arrows came, and then another, each time being met with another wall of soil knocking them from the sky. Marta now had full control of her powers and all could witness this. The tribes' people were now aware of why the land had been good to them and who they should be grateful too. They were also aware that if they made their way to behind Marta, they would be safe and proceeded to do so. Amongst those to witness this were Marta's parents. They began to approach her with bemused wonderment, trying to find the words to express their feelings at what their daughter was doing.

"Mum, Dad, no time to explain, just get yourself safe and trust me."

"Not a chance" shouted Mack, "we will always be by your side baby girl." With that Ava and Mack stood either side of Marta placing their hands upon her shoulders, ready to support and witness all that their daughter was about to do.

The moment her parents placed their hands upon her, Marta felt another surge of power given to her by the support and love. It mixed with the rage and despair that she had felt moments before and created a balance. No longer was she just defending her tribe. Now she was on the attack.

For a brief moment the armies had stalled in their advances. They were looking for orders as how to proceed, aware that the arrows were no longer effective and that they were facing something more than they had anticipated. Marta took advantage of the moment. She summoned her powers and as she did, so the earth began to move. Cracks started to develop in front of the armies. They began to spread deeper and wider across the plane of land, until it reached the now abundant and flowing river that travelled through the tribe's land. The river began to fill the cracks, that Marta had created, forming a moat that the armies could not cross. This created a delay whilst the armies reformed their strategy but this was not over yet. Whilst there was distance between them, the armies weapons could still reach them and achieve their purpose of wiping out the tribe. Marta knew that there was no time to waste and she would now have to use her powers for something she dreaded, the destruction of the army.

Marta summoned her powers and began to move the earth once more; this time on the other side of the moat directly beneath the heavily armed enemy. As she did so, waves of earth began to rise and fall beneath the soldiers, sending them flying in all directions as they were no longer able to establish a foothold on the ground. The screams of the soldiers could be heard as they flew through the air. The injuries and fear of what was happening to them was undeniable. Then, in an instant, Marta split apart the land and all the soldiers and their weapons began to fall into the deep ravines that opened beneath them. None were safe from the raging earthquakes that were decimating their ranks. Once they had fallen into the ravines, the earth then closed them up again, sealing in anyone who was unfortunate enough to have experienced this fate. As this happened Marta could feel the pain of all that were suffering from this agonising end. She had been told by the voice that she would feel the bad that her powers brought and nothing could be worse than experiencing this. But it had to be done. The choice was the survival of her loved ones or those that would seek to destroy them. There was no debate and so she would continue until there was no more danger.

Almost all of the army were swallowed up and what few were left, began to flee in the direction of where they come from. The land continued to rumble as a warning but the noise eventually descended into nothing when it was clear that there was no one left to scare away. There was no evidence left of the armies that were recently there. All that remained was the damage left upon the tribe. Buildings could be repaired but the loss of human life could not be so easily recovered from. There were many injured, dying or already dead. So, despite the victory there was nothing to celebrate. Instead there was just silence, as everyone took in the magnitude of what had just happened; of what they had just witnessed. Marta's powers, which had just saved the tribe, were way beyond anyone's understanding. Was she now to be feared, like Scorpius and his daughter Lyra? Marta herself was weakened by the exertions of what had just occurred and slumped into the arms of her father for support. As she and her parents looked around, they could see that everyone was dumbfounded. No one knew what to say. Eventually, Mack decided to speak.

"It has been quite a day. What started out as a celebration turned into a day to commiserate. We all have a lot of questions but now is probably not the time to ask them. Now is the time to stop and deal with what is needed. We must tend to the injured. We must tend to those we have lost and take time to grieve for them. We need to guard our tribe and keep watch in case they return. I probably have more questions than most. How did my baby girl turn from my princess into a goddess that saved us all? How did this happen? But it is not the time for me to seek answers. It is time to care for those that I love, without question and keep this tribe, this family, together and united. I beg of you all to do the same. Let's repair our world both physically and mentally. Then we can move forward and seek answers and solutions together."

Mack's speech was met with approval by all. Everyone began to deal with the tasks at hand. Some are tasked with guarding the tribe, whilst others set about repairing the damage. Most importantly those who are capable dealt with the wounded and the dead. The most heart wrenching task of all.

Mack lifted Marta into his arms and carried her off to their home. She is barely conscious and exhausted from battle. She would need to rest. There will be a lot of questions about what had happened and how she was able to defeat the armies of Scorpius.

Chapter Five

Scorpius' Palace

Scorpius sat alone. He is deep in thought. His brow was furrowed and clearly his thoughts were troubling. Lyra entered and saw her father, sat contemplating. She moved in front of him and curtsied.

"Good day to you Daddy. You look troubled."

"I am indeed daughter. Whilst the sight of you lifts some of my misery. I am afraid that there is not a lot of good to report, my dear."

"Tell me and maybe I will be able to serve you well and take some of your misery away. I certainly do not wish to see you so unhappy." Lyra placed her hand upon her father in order to comfort him. She lowered herself down until she was sat at her father's feet. She leaned her head in and placed it upon his lap, like a child waiting to be told a bedtime story. She looked up at Scorpius and awaited his response to her show of love. Momentarily Scorpius was relieved of his woes. The love of his child was safe and secure, no matter what.

"News from the armies is not good. The tribe that chose not to share their good fortune with us, is quite clearly controlled by someone with powers. The armies witnessed this person control the very land beneath their feet; creating earthquakes where they stood. Very few escaped with their lives. I may have not been there but I can see what they did not. There is a new evil that would seek to destroy all that we have created. If we do not act others will follow this evil until we are overrun and no more; left scraping for morsels like common beggars on the street."

"Yes Daddy. We must deal with this before it goes too far." Whilst aware of her father's sadness, Lyra knew that this was likely to be what she had been told when she was younger. Others like her, with powers would come. However, this excited Lyra, confident that her own powers were greater than all. She would soon be able to use all that she possessed to conquer others and control them for her own gain. Scorpius began to speak once more.

"I fear that it will soon be time for us to leave the seclusion and safety of this palace. Our armies obviously do not have the knowledge and guile to deal with such a problem. This is just one person, but there may be others. We will need to be quick witted in our thinking in order to deal with those who mean us harm. I doubt many of our commanders have the skills to do this. Therefore, I will need to deal with this myself and direct the troops personally."

"No Daddy, this cannot happen. You are needed here to guide us all. I understand that you cannot trust many of your commanders to be skilful and wise in the time of need but leaving here is not the answer. Who would rule in your place? Could they be trusted? I beg you to think of another way."

"I can see no other my child."

"You do not then see what is in front of you." Lyra rose and stood before him. "I shall seek out those who would harm us. Let me lead the armies and I shall lead them to victory in your name. If those that stand against us have powers, then let them battle against mine. They will be no match! Some may be able to conjure some magic but not as great as mine. Whilst they only have the support of shovels and sticks, I will have the support of the mighty Scorpius. We will find them, we will root them out and defeat them. I beg you dear Father of mine, let me do this for you." Lyra has become very caught up in her speech and was clearly excited by the thought of what she had just proposed. At last she would be able to find those that had powers and bend them to her will.

"My dear daughter, you must forgive me. In wallowing in my own self-pity. You are right, I have not opened my eyes to the obvious. If I cannot be there myself, then my own flesh and blood is just as good. Forgive me my sweet child. My first thought should have been that you are worthy of such a task. Maybe I was being selfish and did not wish to lose you from by my side."

"I shall always be with you Daddy. With my powers we will always be connected to each other, even when I am many miles away. Let me do this, and we will overcome it all." Lyra waited for a response as Scorpius pondered for a moment.

"We shall make it so. You shall rule over the armies and we will crush anyone who defies us. First, we must send out scouts and seek out if there are any more with powers. We will need to find out what they are capable of, see what their weaknesses are. Then with the armies and your powers combined we shall wipe them out."

"Yes, yes Daddy!" Lyra could hardly contain her excitement. She has been waiting for this moment. Now was her chance to make sure that she remained the most powerful of all.

"Come my child, we shall let the people know of my decision. I am assured that they will rejoice at my plan. Then we shall make sure that we are prepared for all that may come. I fear that we have little time to waste. So, we must proceed with our plan at once. Thank you dear Lyra, I would be lost without you. You are my all and my everything."

"As are you to me. Let's make preparations. All will soon see the true power of this kingdom." Lyra was overjoyed at the thought of what would happen and left with her father to ready the troops.

Chapter six

Marta's Next Chapter

It had been a few days since the attack on the tribe and all were slowly recovering from their injuries; whether they were physical or emotional. Marta herself had mainly stayed in bed; firstly, because of the exhaustion of her efforts to fend off the attacking army and secondly, because she feared how everyone would feel about her, having witnessed what happened. Even her own parents had avoided asking her about the events of a few days ago. Conversation had been kept to standard pleasantries and the necessary questions about food and drink. Ava and Mack were very curious indeed to find out how their daughter had such powers but they felt that it was up to Marta to initiate the conversation. She understood this too, yet she was trying to put it off for as long as possible. She was aware that everything had changed now. No longer was she a sweet innocent child that needed the protection of her parents. In fact, quite the opposite. Yet she feared this change, hoping to hold on to last moments she had of being their baby. However, the awkwardness of the delay was becoming too evident and she knew it was time to engage in the conversation that she dreaded. She approached her parents with reticence.

"So, I suppose you have a few questions?"

Ava and Mack looked up from the table that they were sitting at. They both smiled at her lovingly. They were aware that this was not a comfortable moment for their daughter and wished to put her at ease. Mack began to speak.

"Well, when our daughter single-handedly defeats the armies of Scorpius, it does raise a few." As he said this Ava took Marta by the hand and guided her to sit with them both.

"Whatever has happened, you are our daughter and we love you no matter what. So, you tell us what you can. We will understand." Ava adds.

Marta at first was lost for words. How does anyone explain it all?

"So, after I had the long sleep, something changed. First of all I felt fitter and healthier than I ever had. I thought at first that it was just that my recovery had made me that way. But then something else happened. I started hearing a voice, which I thought at first was just me being a bit crazy but then I realised it was something else. The voice wasn't so much in my head but talking to me from somewhere else; really far away, yet sounding like it was coming from right next to me, like you two are now." Marta paused for a moment, realising that as she stumbled to get the words out, they are difficult to understand. "It makes as little sense to me, as I say it, as it probably does to you."

"Your Mum and I gave up wondering about what makes sense, in this crazy world, a long time ago princess. So, I shouldn't worry."

Marta smiled at the thought that, despite all that had happened, she was still her father's little princess. So, she continued to explain.

"The voice started to tell me about things. About what I could do with the earth. Then the voice started to teach me how to do things. You see, I can control the earth. I have a power that allows me to do things and so I did. That's why the land got better. That's why it got better for the tribe. The voice taught me all this. Then when the armies attacked, it got stronger. I think the more I feel something, the stronger my powers get. So, when they attacked, I moved the earth and well, destroyed them." There is a pause and a moment of silence from all of them whilst they took in the magnitude of what had transpired.

"What does this voice say now dearest?" Ava asked.

"Nothing. I haven't spoken to them since the attack. I'm almost afraid too. I'm not sure I was meant to inflict that much damage and pain. I'm afraid to find out. Perhaps I'm in trouble and it might come back on me."

"You saved us." Mack chimed in. "If this voice doesn't realise that, then it's wrong and maybe it needs to leave. Perhaps it should stop talking to you if it doesn't like it."

"I'm not sure it works like that Dad." Marta smiled at her father. He was being protective in a world that he didn't understand. But he would fight to the end regardless, for his daughter.

"Perhaps you should try talking to this voice. It's better to know, rather than spending your day wondering and hiding from it." Ava wisely added "Do you want to try talking to them now, whilst we are with you?"

"No mother, this is something I need to do alone. It's time for me to take responsibility and grow up." Whilst both parents were proud with their daughter, they were also tinged with sadness and concern that their child was growing up and maybe into a world that they couldn't understand or protect her from.

"Ok my dear I think we should leave you in peace. We won't go far, just outside in case you change your mind and decide you need us." Ava replied. She then hustled Mack along, who still wasn't sure, and went outside. Marta then gathered herself before she plucked up enough courage to speak to the voice.

"Are you still there? We should probably talk."

"I never left." Replied the voice. "I was just waiting for when you were ready."

"So you saw what I did."

"I did."

"Well, am I in trouble?"

"Not with me, although there will be trouble ahead."

"Kinda not the answer I was hoping for." Marta responded. "I was hoping that what happened was all that I had to do. You said I had to experience bad as well as the good. Well I've done that now, is it not over?"

"There is much still to do. This was just the first of many battles. There are many places suffering in this world that need help. Your powers can help many and as a result there will always be those that seek to destroy something that they do not understand. Right now even your own people fear you. But they will understand. Particularly after what will happen next. Then you will have to seek out others like you. They can help on the next stage of your journey."

"Journey? Since when am I going anywhere?" Marta exclaimed.

"You cannot remain here. Those that seek to destroy you will return to find you. If you stay, you will put at risk all that you care for deeply. You must travel great distances. Seek out those that can help you. Many people will need your help and alone you will fail. Once you have found the ones that contain the power of the wind, the fire and water, you must then seek me out. I shall guide you on your way, just as I have guided the others."

"Great." Marta said sarcastically. "So there's no chance you could make it easy and come and meet us instead. Just saying."

"I am not free and cannot meet you. You must seek me out, when you have found the others. Only then can I be freed."

"Ok, maybe you should have mentioned something about you not being free before. This is all beginning to sound a bit dodgy. So just find people that can control wind, water and fire. Then come and get you from whatever hellhole you are in. Yeah, no problem." Marta's sarcasm was evident as she began to realise the magnitude of her responsibilities. "And what about my people? Surely they are going to need my help too. I can't just leave them and expect them to be ok."

"You will make sure that they are safe before you leave." Replied the voice. "I shall guide you in preparing for your journey. For now you must rest. There will be a great deal to do and it will use a lot of your strength just to complete tomorrow's tasks, before your travels begin. Today will be your last full day with your tribe, for tomorrow a new life begins."

Marta paused for a moment to take in what had just been said. She could see no positives in what would happen but knew that she must do it.

"Will I ever see my family again after tomorrow?" She asked.

"There is hope that you will one day return but success cannot be guaranteed."

"That's what I thought. I was kinda hoping for a different answer, I'm not going to deny it. I suppose I should have known that these powers were going to come at a price. Why me though? Couldn't you have chosen a bit better?"

"The choice was made and I believe it to be a good one." replied the voice.

"Ok. Can you leave me alone for now? I would like to spend some time with my parents while I can."

"Of course."

Marta sat for a moment. She had a lot to think about. Her parents came in. Despite the fact that they were going to leave her alone, they had been listening in at the door.

"We have a lot to talk about." Marta said.

"We know." Ava responded, fighting back the tears in her eyes. Although, she could only hear one half of the conversation, she had a general understanding of what had been said and what was about to happen.

"You heard then?" Marta too was on the verge of tears. They all embraced each other, not wanting to ever let go, aware that the next few hours would be precious and potentially the last that they would share together.

Chapter Seven

A New Day

Marta woke early. There was much to be done today. She had relished every moment with her parents the night before, fearing it to be the last. But now it was time to prepare for the future. Time to forget about the past and create a better life for all. In order to do this she would have to sacrifice herself. She would need to leave behind those that she loved and set off to create a new world. She was prepared, she understood that her powers meant that this was her destiny.

She arranged with her father that he would gather together the tribe. She needed to address them, in order to put their minds at rest and convince them that what she would do today, was for the best. But first she had to do something for herself. Something that was likely to be painful but needed to be done for her own peace of mind. She walked through the tribe until she arrived at a tented home that she knew well. She was afraid to go in, fearing that she may not be welcome and worried about what she might find. This was the home of Rags and his family. Since the attack he had remained unconscious and was not doing well in his recovery. She called out as she pulled back the doorway and entered. There stood Rags' parents. There was a moment of hesitation between everyone. Marta wondered if they blamed her for the state that Rags was in. However, as she moved further into their dwelling Rags' parents embraced her, putting everyone at ease.

"How is he?" Asked Marta.

"Not much has changed since he was shot. We had to remove the arrow, which meant he lost a lot of blood. He hasn't regained consciousness yet. We are hoping that something changes but we will just have to wait." Rags' father replied.

"I'm so sorry! I wish I could do something. I'm surprised you even want me here." Marta responded, whilst holding back the tears and trying to maintain some sort of composure.

"Don't be silly, you saved us all young lady. Rags adores you and was at his happiest when this happened. You will always be welcome in our house. So, no tears, go and sit with him a while and hopefully he will know you're there and it will do some good." Marta followed the dad's instructions and sat beside the stricken Rags. She took his hand in hers and composed herself.

"How you doing my daft friend? You've got to get better for me. I mean, all this time and we finally realise we like each other more than we realised.

How silly is that? So we've both got something we need to do. You need to get better and while you're doing that I've got to go off and save the world, apparently." Marta had a nervous laugh at what she had just said. "See, so I haven't exactly got it easy whilst you rest up. You'd better get yourself sorted, because I'm hoping that one day I will return and you will be waiting for me. Which means no other girls, is that clear? I'm not giving you a free pass, just because I might never return." Marta tried to keep it light hearted, not just for Rags but for her own peace of mind. "Seriously though, I don't really mind what you get up to. But I have to admit I'm a bit scared. Not just about what I have to do, but even if I do manage to achieve everything out there, what happens back here? Will you all be waiting when I return? Will my parents be ok? Will you be better? Will you still like me when I get back? I've just met my guy and now I have to leave and he's not even able to say goodbye to me. Have I met the man that I'm meant to spend the rest of my life with only to go away and let him forget me? Anyway I'm just rambling on now. I've got used to talking to myself. I will have to tell you about that some other time." She paused for moment. "Just get better. Give me something extra to return home for." She kissed him tenderly and then laid down beside him. She decided to take a moment to remember all the good times that they had together and cherish them.

After a while she got up and took one last look at him. She bade his parents farewell and headed off. This was to be a monumental day and there was still so much to do.

Marta then headed off to find the main bulk of the tribe that have gathered together at her request. She thought it best to talk to everyone in order to ease any tension that may have arisen, from them witnessing her powers. Also, today they would witness even more of her skills and she needed to make them aware of what was going to happen. As the large group gathered, she took a moment to think of the words she needed to say. She climbed up on top of a table with the assistance of her Dad. She took a moment to look out amongst the crowd that had gathered. So many faces, all of which she cherished. The tribe had been through so much and they had survived the hardest of times. All these people were as much responsible for her upbringing as her parents. Without them she would not have survived the tough day to day life that they had endured. Now it was her time to help them. To make life easier. She needed them to understand that despite the recent attack, she could make everything better for them. She needed them to trust her. She began to speak.

"Hey everybody, it's been a bit crazy recently and you probably have a few questions. I would like to answer them but to be honest I don't have an answer to them all. There is a lot of stuff I'm not sure of myself. As you saw, I have developed some powers. These powers let me control the earth beneath our feet. I don't know why I have these powers or how I got them, I just have. Until we got attacked I had kept them a secret. Not even my parents knew about them. So, they don't have any answers either. All I can say is that, for the most part these powers are good. I used them to play with the land that we live on and made things better for us all. That's all I thought I would do until we were attacked. Up until that point I was happy keeping it a secret and everyone believing that it was just good fortune. I was happy and I believe that you were too. But then the armies of Scorpius came and I had to do something. I couldn't just let the people I loved, you, be hurt. They wanted to wipe us out, to kill us. So, I had to do something about it. I am not proud of what I had to do. The pain that I caused, even to those that were trying to harm us, is something that I will have to live with. Something that will haunt me until I die. I hope that you, the people that I consider family, my people, my tribe, can forgive me for what happened." Marta looked out at the crowd. She was afraid that they might reject her or condemn her for her actions. She was however, reassured by the looks she was receiving. There was a general look of acceptance as if they are satisfied with what she did in order to save them. She heard a murmur of contentment coming from the tribe. The feeling flowing towards her, was that of love. Of a collective, willing to support and appreciate her. Ava reached up, squeezed her daughter's hand and smiled at her, as she realised that all was good. Marta knew she had the support to continue.

"So what happens now? I don't think that I will be left alone now. Scorpius will be aware of what happened to his army and he will want revenge. It wouldn't be fair on you if I stayed, because it is me that he will come looking for. By staying, I will put you in danger. There is also a lot I can do in this world by using this power to help others. So, that is what I must do." Marta looked down at her parents. The sadness was filling up within them as they realised that it wouldn't be long before they must say goodbye to their daughter. However, they realised this was a sacrifice that they had to make for the greater good. Marta smiled at them reassuringly before she carried on.

"Before I leave, I will use my powers once more to create a safe place for you. I shall mould the land to create a fortress. You will live within that fortress and remain safe. No one will be able to break into it but also no one will be able to leave. I shall make sure that the land inside will be fertile enough for all to live for decades. You will all be safe, it will be a world within the world. You will be able to live happy and free. You will never have to worry about anything or anyone for the rest of your days." The murmuring from the tribe continued as they discussed, amongst themselves, what was going to happen. Still everyone remained content. The world has been harsh for so long and the idea of living without troubles could at last become a reality.

"One day I hope I will be able to return. I don't know when this might be. Hopefully, it will be when everything is alright with the world and it is safe to come back. I hope when that happens that everyone will be safe and well. I hope that I can one day return to live a happy and normal life with you all. Hopefully I can grow old, have kids and just behave like an idiot or something. Maybe one day. But for now I have a lot to do. So gather everyone together here by the river in one hour and then the changes will begin."

For a moment everyone was motionless before what has just been said sank in. Then everyone started to move at speed, realising that a lot was about to change very soon and they had better make sure that they were not in the way of what Marta was about to do. Marta sat down on the table that she had been standing on. She watched as the tribe scurried about, making sure that there were no stragglers or children hiding away where they could get hurt. Livestock was moved towards the river to ensure their safety. Finally, the wounded from the attack are moved to join the large group gathering together, this of course included Rags. Marta moved over to him in order to hold his hand and spend her last moments with him.

In time everything was sorted and the tribe was ready for what was about to happen. Marta's parents had remained close by and placed their hands on her shoulders in support, just as they had during the attack. Marta looked at them and began to speak.

"You must join the rest of the tribe now. I can feel your love without you being with me."

Marta's parents did as they are told. They hugged their daughter and joined the rest of the tribe. Marta then moved to the edge of all the makeshift homes in order to give herself a clearer view of everything. She began to talk to the voice, in order to seek as much support as possible.

"Here goes, I hope I can do this."

"You are ready." The voice replies. "Think of all the love within the tribe for you. They wish you nothing but success. They believe in you and would not judge you harshly. If you feel all that love and belief then you will not fail."

"Ok. I can do this." Marta bolstered herself up and then concentrated; focusing on the love and belief from the tribe. Then she channelled that into making changes to the surroundings. First, she felt the earth beneath her feet. She felt the soil and the moisture below. She spread out and felt all the life waiting to burst from the ground below. She felt it all. She was bonded together with it and it gave her life, strength, power. The connection was strong and limitless. She knew she could do whatever she needed to and started to instruct the earth to do what she desired. First, she began to move the hills and mountains that surrounded the tribe. She moved them out further to give them more space to live. As she did this, the mountains rose higher into the sky, to protect from any would be invaders. Then she stretched them around the tribe; sealing them in from both sides, making sure there are no entrances or exits, forming a fortress of protection. On the inside of the circle of mountains, that now surround them, they are sloped up to the top so that anyone from the tribe can climb them but on the outside, there was a sheer drop, with a smooth face, impossible to climb and too high for anyone to attach a rope to. When seen from the outside it would appear as if someone had built a smooth marble wall and would not even attempt to climb it.

By moving the mountains back, she had created acre upon acre of clear land for the tribe to live. At the moment this land was barren so Marta needed to make them fertile for farming. The river had now been blocked by the circle of mountains. So, she buried deep into the land, providing a well of water coming from down below. This would be a constant source and couldn't be tampered with, from the outside of the fortress. Now that she had a constant water supply, Marta began to move the earth into streams that looped all around the newly created land. This would give an easy access to the water and make it easier to farm the land. She also pulled moisture and plant life, buried deep within the soil, to create greenery and to begin the circle of life for this new world. Marta began to break off the connection between herself and the earth. She had created a beautiful and safe world for her tribe. All are amazed at what they had witnessed and the excitement was overflowing amongst all the people. Marta gathered herself and walked down to join them. As she arrived there was a moment of awkwardness between herself and the tribe. Having seen what Marta had just created, no one was quite sure how to respond. Their own Marta, child of the tribe, had done the work of a God. It was not easy to treat her as an ordinary person. Yet this was what Marta was waiting for, what she craved. Marta's parents approached and embraced her tightly.

"It's wonderful." Ava exclaimed.

"Don't you be thinking that just because you can do all this and create a whole new world, that you're not still our little girl and can get away with everything" Mack joked.

"I won't Dad. I'm still your princess." Marta was happy that they had responded in this way. She wished for nothing more than being an ordinary teenager but it was never likely to be that way ever again. She knew that much greater tasks lay ahead and she had to leave in order to achieve that. She looked on at all the excited and happy faces that surrounded her for one last time.

"I have to go now." She looked at her parents who were starting to well up with tears, just as Marta was herself.

"I've put as much in it as I can. Hopefully, it will keep you going for a while." Ava said as she handed her daughter a rucksack full of provisions. "Now that you've done all this and we are safe, I don't understand why you have to go. Can't you just stay?"

"I wish I could Mother but there are lots of other people and tribes that need me. I was given this power for a reason."

"I understand. Please come home one day."

"I will, I promise." Marta then embraced her parents again. They all held each other as tight as they could.

Eventually Marta tore herself away from her sobbing Mother and a father that was trying to tough it out but failing dismally as the tears rolled down his face. She picked up the rucksack and walked towards the edge of the fortress she had created. As she approached the mountainous terrain a tunnel opened up before her. She reached the opening and turned around to take one last look at the loved ones she was leaving behind. She entered the tunnel and travelled through the mountain range to the outside of the fortress. When she reached the outside world, she closed the tunnel once more, keeping her tribe safe from the world outside. She then began her epic journey that the voice had instructed her to take. She was to help many others like her tribe and she was going seek out others, like her, with powers. Today was the beginning of a new life for all.

Chapter Eight

Marta's Journey

Over time, Marta began to carry out the instructions of the voice. All along she received further training on her powers, making it easier to use them. Each time, the bond between herself and the earth would become stronger, as the powers flowed much more easily through her. She travelled far, searching for other tribes along her way. Each time she found one she would seek out the elders or the leaders. First, she would give a small display of her skills, gaining trust from the people. Little by little she would show them more, being careful not to scare anyone. Eventually, she would display the extent of her powers and create a safe home for all, just like she had done with her own tribe. When she had completed all that she wished, she would move on and seek out another settlement to help. She was creating fortresses across the land, keeping the people safe and healthy. Each time the tribes would be extremely grateful and hoped that she would stay with them forever. But each time Marta moved on, taking just enough provisions to keep her going until she found her next tribe.

Word was starting to pass throughout the world, of this wondrous child of the earth that was coming to save them. As such, Marta had to take many precautions as she travelled around; aware that armies of Scorpius were beginning to seek her out. When she was not staying with a tribe, she would create a home, by surrounding herself with earth and rocks; this allowed her to rest and eat without being disturbed. Although, if she had come across any armies, she had dealt with them. She did not want to cause any more pain and suffering. She also did not wish to create a pattern of her whereabouts. So, she travelled and created fortresses in a random manner, always staying one step ahead of those that would track her down. This continued for many months and over great distances, until one day the routine changed.

Marta had just climbed up a mountainous range. She reached the top and could see for miles around her. The view was breath taking. Despite the harsh conditions that most lived in this world, it was still beautiful. One day she hoped it would all be healed and be a wonderful home for everyone once more. In the distance she could see the remains of what was once a great city.

"It is time to rest." Said the voice.

"Ok, give me a moment and I shall create some barriers." responded Marta.

"Do not do that. This time you must be seen." Marta was surprised at what the voice just said.

"That's not usual. And there is an old city in the distance, there are bound to be troops around here."

"Exactly."

"I never understand your plans. I have spent all this time creating safe places for everyone, which by the way I would have been quite happy to stay at and relax; especially that one with the nice waterfall I created and now you're saying you want me to just chill out here until maybe I see some army people."

"Yes."

"Brilliant! So I will just sit here and chill then. You can be really annoying sometimes. Do you know that?"

"Yes, I know." The voice began to chuckle. "The waterfall was nice though. One day you will return to all the wonderful places you have created."

"Really. I will return to all these places? Assuming I don't die along the way."

"Well assuming you don't die. I forgot that bit." Replied the voice in an amusing tone.

"You're such an idiot sometimes!" Marta responded. "Why did I even do all that stuff? I could be taking it easy at home if it wasn't for you!"

"I understand that you are making a huge sacrifice but it is all important and will be worthwhile. Whether we succeed or not, all those people will have a better and healthier life. One day they may be needed to create a new world. If everyone is already broken then there may be nothing left to fix in the future."

"Wow you really are a bundle of laughs sometimes." Marta replied. "If we ever actually meet I am going to have to teach you something about saying the right things in the right moment."

"I look forward to the day we meet. If it happens it will be a brighter day for all. Until then there is still so much to do."

"Excellent. What's next then? You've got me waiting up here. What's the next move?"

"Watch and all will become clear."

"Ok. You're the boss. I think."

Marta did not have to wait long. In the distance she could see the winds beginning to swirl around the city. They were becoming stronger and more rapid. Forming tornadoes that appeared to sweep in and out of the city, targeting various spots.

"Something is happening over in the city!" Marta exclaimed.

"It is and you need to be ready."

Marta steadied herself. By now she was getting used to her powers and could easily use them at a moment's notice. She could see that the winds were intensifying in and around the city. This was no longer a chance happening but something much stronger than that. There seemed to be a greater power at play all of a sudden and Marta needed to be on her guard, in case anything started to move her way. Then it did!

All of a sudden there was a burst of action exploding from the city. The winds had blown up clouds of dust and dirt and through it a mass of troops were beginning to emerge. Most were on horseback charging out of the city towards where Marta was based. An endless rampage of heavily armed troops, were seemingly heading right for her. Marta was unaware of what had caused this. Why were they coming towards her? Surely her presence had not caused this. One lone girl standing on top of a mountain. Whatever it was, she would soon be in grave danger and would need to act.

"Wait a moment." Said the voice. "They are not aware of you yet. They will only need to be stopped, not hurt in any way."

"Ok, are you sure? Because that looks very much like a big angry mob coming to get me."

"It is not you they seek. Take your time. Wait for them to clear the city then open up the earth in front of them, to stop their charge."

Marta did as instructed by the voice. She waited for the rampaging army to clear some distance from the city. This left them in a large open plain of land before the mountain range, where Marta was based. When she realised the time was right she opened up the earth in front of them, creating a deep gully in the earth. The armies slowed as they approached, realising that the land had suddenly become impossible to traverse. Slowly, the energy of the army began to disperse and the troops began to look for orders from their higher ranks. The senior officers approached the deep gully, to witness for themselves what had just happened. They then signalled for the bulk of the troops to return to the city, whilst the more senior officers remained.

It was then that Marta realised what had caused the troops to charge out of the city. They were not just looking at the newly formed gully ,that had miraculously just formed before them but they were also looking up into the sky. As the dust began to settle, the view became clearer. One person had made it over the deep gully and was heading towards Marta. This was clearly who the troops were chasing. A young man barely into adulthood was coming towards Marta. He was coming at great speed and clearly escaping the troops. However, this was no ordinary young man. He had made it away from the troops and over the gully for one very good reason. He was flying!

Chapter Nine

Wind

No date, no time, no location. A once great city; ravaged by the harsh world, now used as an internment camp. This was a place that no one wanted to live. The only way to survive was to keep your head down and do as you were told. Once beautiful and towering skyscrapers, crumbled away under the constant battering of the harsh world surrounding them. Streets that were once bustling commercial outlets, were now no more than shelter for the inhabitants. Places to sleep, to survive, living out the miserable existence of a pitiful life. Each day the troops come round to herd up the people and march them off to outside of the city. There they are made to work the land or mine down below. Their purpose was not to create a living for themselves but to provide for the troops and to create resources for Scorpius and all his followers. The meagre amounts that are left are given to the inhabitants of the city. If the hard work didn't kill you, the hunger would. A wretched life for all. Memories of when it was a thriving metropolis were distant ago and were likely make you even more unhappy.

However, not all lived down in the streets. One mother and her son lived high in the skyscrapers, away from everyone. Hidden from the troops that would put them to work. The son was a young adult, approaching full manhood. He was a tall, thin lad, with a pale complexion and a mass of blond hair. He was called Sam and lived with his mother, Lucy, high up in the tower. From there they could witness all that was happening below and given that no one risks climbing up the skyscrapers anymore, they were safe from the troops. They lived a comfortable lifestyle in comparison to those down below, as they lived in the remains of what was once a very luxurious apartment. There was no power. So, heat and cooking fuel was provided for by anything they could burn; usually furniture from the abandoned neighbouring apartments. It was a lonely life for the two of them but better than being enslaved by the troops down below. During the day they searched around the higher levels of the buildings for resources; out of sight from all, clear of any danger. At night Sam ventured down to street level to acquire food, using his own special techniques. Sam was no ordinary young man. Sam had skills. Sam had powers.

Sam could control the wind. He learned of his skills through a voice in his head and he had been using those skills to keep himself and his mother safe. He soon realised that no one kept a record of who was in the city. If people didn't turn up for work details they were assumed dead. The only known way of getting the meagre supply of food was hard labour. So, everyone usually turned up, regardless of how awful it was. Therefore, he and his mother could disappear high up into the towers and no one would notice or care. They could remain safe and comfortable there, as rarely does anyone look up in this city; only down at the floor whilst they cursed their miserable lives. At night Sam would come down to the ground and use his powers to their advantage. By using the wind, he could move any size of object that was in his way. More importantly he had adapted his skill to give him something that would be of great use. He could fly. Sam always wore a long coat, which he had adapted by inserting lightweight but strong poles through the seams, scavenged from other buildings. By placing his hands into the pockets and stretching out the coat, he could create wings for flight. He could then control the winds to move him in any direction he desired. This made his skills formidable and easy to use at any time. Even if anyone had the vaguest of reason to suspect that there was anything suspicious going on, Sam could easily disappear, at a moments' notice, high into the sky and back to where his mother was hidden.

Today was like any other to Sam. He had searched through the old, abandoned apartments and found a few interesting items. In one he had found some board games, which were always a treasured find. With these he and his mother would spend hours of enjoyment, escaping from the realities of the world.

In another, plenty of barely worn clothing in his mothers' size, enough to keep her happy for a while. In a world where having a wash was a luxury, a change of clothes was always welcome. After his daytime scavenging was done Sam rested, preparing himself for his evening plans. When night fell, Sam would begin to execute his evening routine.

Sam would descend down to ground level. Sometimes he would float down. Sometimes he would just take the stairs, depending on his mood or how many troops were still patrolling around the city. Then he would seek out supplies. He would never take from the inhabitants, their resources were slim enough already. He would always take from the stores of the armies, as they always had enough for themselves and a surplus to send off to Scorpius and his followers.

Sam arrived at the troops' encampment ready to enact his plan. By now this was a well-practised routine, enough to gain the required supplies without raising the alarm. He knew in which tents everything was kept and it was easy enough to acquire the goods he needed. Troops were always on guard but he could easily manipulate their movements using his powers. Sam approached the required spot and then started to make the winds swirl. The winds then became stronger, knocking tents about and forcing troops to change their movements in order to avoid the strong gusts. When all the troops had moved into his desired positions he would act. Sam then increased the ferocity of the wind, making it swirl and blast through the camp. The power of this wind would be enough uproot one of the tents, sending all the troops into a panic as they rushed to save the tent, and all that was within, from blowing away. All the time they would be cursing the constant winds that caused this to happen most nights. Sam had been smart and never attacked the same tent twice. That way the troops assumed it was just the weather conditions of the area where they were encamped. It also gave Sam the opportunity to uncover randomly selected tents and discover what was beneath them. Whilst the troops were distracted, trying to save the stricken tent, Sam would sweep into action. He would extend out his coat and use the winds to direct him towards his desired destination, the supplies tent. By now this would be unguarded as the troops had rushed to help in the rescue attempt. Swiftly, Sam would move in and begin to raid the supplies tent, taking as much as he could, as quickly as he could; filling up as many bags as he could carry and sustain his flight. Never was he too greedy or did he take an excessive amount of one particular item. His aim was to go unnoticed and therefore he needed to leave everything looking very similar to before, that way no one would suspect that they had been raided whilst they left their post. Then, as swiftly as he had arrived, he would leave. Taking to the skies he would return to his mother, providing her with a feast of resources to help her survive.

"Thank you, Sam." Lucy said on his return. She was proud of her son and his achievements but feared that this would not last forever. They could not spend the rest of their days hiding in the shadows and Sam could not always look after his Mother. She understood that he had been blessed with these powers and they were meant for greater things other than scavenging in the dark. "You need to do something other than just look after me you know."

"Don't be silly Mum, there is nothing I'd rather be doing. Do we have everything we need?"

"Yes dear."

"Cool. Well you just take it easy then Mum, I'm going to head back up to the roof and chill for a bit. See you later." Sam embraced his mum and headed out of their apartment. He took the stairs up to the roof. When he arrived there, he sat with his legs over the edge of the rooftop, where he can see all that went on below. He witnessed the flicker from fires lit around the city. Around them were gathered the inhabitants, trying to gain some warmth whilst huddled tightly together. The fires cast light and shadow onto the once great buildings that are now empty shadows of their former selves. Now, just empty boxes stacked on top of each other. Sam did not know any different from this current life. What vague memories he had, were very distant and seemed more like his own imagination rather than a reality that once happened. Occasionally, the inhabitants around the fires would share stories and songs to keep up morale. Sam would listen to these, with interest, from his perch way up high. Although they were often tales of better times past, they acted to create calm and a sense of hope to those that listened. Suddenly there was a sound that disturbed Sam's peace.

"Your Mother is right you know." Spoke the voice.

"Great, I wondered when I would hear from your cheery voice again. And what is my Mum right about?" replied Sam.

"Your powers have greater uses than just stealing food in the night. You are meant for greater things and soon you will have to move on from this life."

"What if I don't want to? Are these powers going to leave me?"

"The choice unfortunately will be made for you soon enough. Neither you nor I have control over that."

"What about my Mum?"

"Her life will unfortunately change but that is her path. Perhaps one day her path and yours will come together again and all will be good but I cannot say for certain."

"She's my Mum! I need a better guarantee than that!"

"I'm sorry but that is the best I can say."

"Just leave me alone! I understand that I have these powers but right now I am not listening to your rubbish. So, you might as well clear off and bother someone else." Sam was exasperated at the exchange with the voice and began to stomp around the rooftop trying to shake out the sound of the voice.

"As you wish I shall leave for now."

Sam let out a long sigh as he realised that he was now completely alone. He headed back to the edge of the rooftop and prepared himself to take flight. Nothing created the feeling of freedom, in Sam, more than flying and right now not having a care in the world was exactly what he needed. He stretched out and caught the wind that he had created. He pushed himself off and he was weightless and free once more. The bond between himself and the wind was strong. Not only did the wind hold him in the air but it also passed its energy into him and Sam could feel as carefree as he wished. It was almost as though it cleansed him from all the worries and exertions of the world.

Sam soared higher and began to circle around the city, watching over all that was happening below. It was quiet, as everybody was beginning to try and get as much rest as possible. When daylight came around once more, the inhabitants would be gathered up to work for the armies. There were no rest days here, no break from the routine, no new places to go in this unforgiving world.

No date, no time, no location.

As he soared high and out of sight Sam began to forget the conversation with the voice. He couldn't be forced into leaving his mother and worrying about it was seemingly pointless. Sam was free and he was happy.

CHAPTER TEN

The Inevitable

As Sam soared above the city, he enjoyed the tranquillity. He could not be seen or heard and was safe from the stresses of the world below. No one to worry about, as most were just trying to rest. His mother was fed and asleep. Nothing but pure freedom. As he floated, carefree through the skies, he could feel the energy that the wind was giving him. Added to the peace and serenity he was feeling, Sam was on a high. As he felt more relaxed, Sam began to play in the air, testing his skills. He could sweep in and out of the high-rise buildings, testing his skills of manoeuvring; all the time making his turns sharper and tighter. The more challenging it got the greater his rush of excitement. He was happy to play like this all night long, until the sun began to rise.

Suddenly a sound broke Sam's serenity. A cry piercing through the night. Worse still, this was a continuous cry of a child. Sam circled around the city to find where it was coming from. Eventually, he spied a small girl, walking through the debris of a collapsed building, looking for someone she knew. She was clearly lost, wandering the dark streets in search of her family and Sam decided that he should help. He flew down and landed nearby. He did not wish to scare her and he made sure that he was slightly out of sight from her when he landed.

He approached her to find out what the problem was and how he could help.

"Hey there little girl, what's the problem?" Sam asked. "Have you lost your family?"

The girl was too upset to speak and slightly wary of this young man who had just appeared. She nodded in reply to his question.

"Ok I know it's a bit scary. So, why don't we go look around for them. You just point where you want to go and I will come with you. Hopefully, we will find them. Is that ok?"

The girl nodded again and cheered up slightly at the thought of not being alone. She could see that he was not one of the troops and was slightly happier with him being there. She began to walk in the direction of where she thought her family might be and Sam walked beside her whilst they searched the deserted streets.

After a while they came to an area that the girl seemed more familiar with. She pointed to a building that she recognised and moved swiftly towards it. It was an old, abandoned grocery shop, the type that in olden times would have sold everything that anyone needed. Outside stood a woman, who was quite clearly distraught and looking for something or someone. As they approached the shop the child called out.

"Mummy!" and she ran towards the distraught woman who was evidently the child's mother. They embraced and there was a mixture of tears. Some from the anguish that they had experienced and some tears of joy from being reunited.

"Thank you so much. She must of just walked out the front door and got lost in the dark." The mother exclaimed. "Please do come inside and get yourself warm. The winds are very harsh tonight."

Sam was hesitant. Not only because he did not have much experience in dealing with people other than his mother but he was also aware that the harsh winds that she was talking about were created by him. He had not considered before that his pastime of flying around may have caused some discomfort to those on the ground.

"Thank you. If you are sure it's not any trouble." Sam replied as he thought it might be rude to refuse her invitation.

Sam entered the shop front that was now empty of any stock. What was once there, was long gone and used up. He was then guided out to the back where a makeshift home had been made in what were once the storage rooms. Several people lay on makeshift beds, some fashioned from mattresses taken from the homes that once existed in this area. Some lay on materials and blankets, placed on the floor. Quite clearly there were several families living here together, sharing everything they had with one another. Sam quickly became aware that many were sick and starving; barely surviving in an old rotten building. He realised that in comparison he was very healthy and in much better condition than all those that surrounded him and it shook him to the core.

"Would you like something to eat or drink? We don't have much but it's the least we could do for finding our daughter."

"No really that's not necessary. In fact I really should go before my own Mum misses me." Sam replied quickly. How could he take anything from these people who had so little and lived in such squalid conditions? All he wanted to do was get out of there. He smiled at the girl, he had found, and walked back through the shop to the front door. This was just a short trip but on the way out it seemed like a lifetime, as the guilt at what he had just seen weighed heavily on his shoulders. As he got to the door he opened it and bolted out into the street. He then turned the corner and found a safe place where no one could see him. He summoned the winds, launched himself up into the skies and back towards his own home, which now seemed like a palace in the skies compared to what he had just seen.

Sam landed on the rooftop and tried to gather his thoughts. This was what the voice had been talking about. How could he have been so selfish? All this time he had not considered anyone but himself and his mother. People were suffering and he was not using his powers to help. He needed to take action. There was a reason that he could do what he could do and he needed to do something about it. As the sun rose on a new day, Sam sat and thought about his plan of action. No more would he waste what he had been given. It was time to help everyone. He then went to check on his mum, knowing his next decision would affect her life too.

He returned to the apartment and saw his mother sleeping. How could he tell her that he might have to leave her? This woman had cared for him for so long and he had done his best to help her too. They had been a strong team and had survived through all the turmoil, yet it might be time to be apart from each other. Maybe it would just be temporary but it could also be permanent. Sam decided the best thing to do was write a note. If he woke her his decision might be swayed by her and he was determined to stay on the path that he was about to choose. He gathered together some paper and a pencil, that he had scavenged on one of his previous forays, and he hastily wrote a note to his mother. He then placed it in a position that she would find it when she woke up. He hoped she would understand. He hoped he would make her proud. He took one last look at her and then returned to the rooftop to begin his plan of action.

When he arrived at the edge of the roof, he took some deep breaths and readied himself. Today was to be the day when everything changed; when his powers would be clear for all to see and he would no longer be a secret. It was daylight and there would be nowhere to hide. He expanded his coat, drew up the winds and dived into them. The troops were readying themselves to gather up the people in the city and make them begin another hard days' toil. This was Sam's target and it was time to make them pay for all the hardship and anguish they had caused.

He swooped down towards the troops' encampment. Now was the time to seek revenge. No more would he have to witness families huddled and starving, barely able to feed their children. Today was his chance to change all this, to feed the people and make the armies suffer. He landed within the fencing that surrounded the camp. This was not the first time he had done this but it was the first time he could be seen. As he landed the troops immediately started making towards him, aware that someone flying into their camp like this was far from normal and could likely be hostile. Sam summoned the winds and at once began to attack the troops; blowing them around like ragdolls, throwing them from their feet and up against the fences surrounding them. The troops struggled to move themselves, pinned as they were against any solid surface, like glue. Once he had removed the troops from his path, Sam strode towards where all the supplies were kept. Anything and everything, was fair game. Whatever he found would be useful for the city inhabitants. The plan was simple, take everything from the troops and send it all around the city and allow the inhabitants to help themselves. One by one Sam lifted every tent or temporary building within the camp; the wind tearing apart the exteriors like tissue paper. Once each building's contents were exposed Sam used the winds to blow it all up and out of the camp, distributing it around the city for collection. Food, clothes, bedding and most of all weapons. Sam could hear the noise of the people rising in volume as they realised that their salvation was arriving. No longer was Sam just destroying the army of Scorpius, he was allowing the people to create their own. Bit by bit, as he tore down one regime he was building another in the hope that they would be able to keep themselves safe and, more importantly, his mother.

Sam began to revel in all that he was doing; enjoying the ever-increasing excitement that was buzzing around the city. The more he could hear the people's joy the more he increased the levels of the winds and sent the supplies further and faster. However, Sam had not thought about how much of a toll it was taking on himself. He was so caught up in it all, feeding on the excitement and taking everything to the extreme for entertainment, that he had not realised he was draining himself and his concentration. Whilst revelling in all that he was doing, he had stopped pinning the troops back, in order to distribute supplies. The troops had now started to gather themselves and readied their weapons. Suddenly there was bang and a sharp whistling sound. He was being shot at! Some troops had managed to take aim and fire. Fortunately, there was still enough wind to make the aim weak and miss but now was the time to change action before one was lucky enough to hit. Time to get out of here and fast.

Sam changed the directions of the wind. He realised he was going to have to take flight quickly and high enough to avoid any more weapons. He extended out his coat and flew high into the sky. He took a look around the city and witnessed the inhabitants gathering up all that he had sent them. He also realised that they could see him and were becoming aware of what had caused their good fortune. He was overjoyed that he had been able to do this but was also aware that he needed to draw the troops away in order to give them time to organise themselves and form an army of their own. Sam took a few passing sweeps at the troops, diving low and taunting them. Sweeping in and out at rapid speeds and avoiding their attempts to shoot him from the skies. When he was sure that he had the undivided attention of all of them, he tempted them into chasing after him. In the distance Sam could see a range of hills and mountains. If he could lead the armies towards them and out of the city, this would surely give the inhabitants time to sort themselves out. Sure enough, with a few more taunting sweeps towards and away from them, the troops began to follow his path. Within the city Sam was able to fly amongst the buildings, giving him enough cover from their weapons but he was aware, as reached the edge of the city limits, he was going to have to rely on speed alone to avoid being hit and captured.

As he reached the edge of the city, he focused on the mountain range ahead. This was his target. He needed to stay close enough to keep their attention but not enough to be caught. The troops themselves had become more focused and had gathered themselves from the shock of being attacked. They were so used to being in control and everyone obeying them without question, that this was a new situation, one that they were not used to. The horseback riders led the charge, maintaining a ferocious speed in their pursuit of Sam. He dared not look back or pause for a moment to see what was happening. The thunderous noise of the pursuit made him all too aware of how close they were getting. He must not falter. He must get to the cover of the hills and mountains or all his efforts would be wasted. The dust being thrown up, not just from the winds that Sam was creating but also the pursuing troops, was becoming unbearable and was beginning to choke and blind Sam. Just a bit further Sam thought. I need to buy time for the people to sort themselves out. Failure was not an option. Closer and closer they seemed to get, firing into the air at Sam. Their aim was getting nearer and Sam was running out of time. The mountains seemed so far away and they were now in open land making him a much easier target. As much as Sam concentrated to make the winds take him faster, he was losing energy and as such his connection with the winds. It was surely, only going to be moments before he could sustain it no longer. He had never used his powers to this extent before and it was beginning to take its toll on him. Barring a miracle, Sam was about to lose this battle. It would only take a moment before he was hit.

The rumble from behind him became louder on the dirt began to fly up into the air with increasing ferocity. Surely they must be almost upon him and he was about to fail in his endeavours but all of a sudden he realised that they were no longer firing at him. What had happened? Why were there no more shots flying towards him? Sam paused for a moment and floated in the air to witness what was going on. It was then that he realised that the increased noise and dirt was not from the pursuing troops but that, all of a sudden, the earth had opened up. It had formed a huge gulley right in front of the chasing armies, stranding them right where they were. Sam didn't waste a moment of this opportunity and turned back towards the mountains. He needed rest and somewhere to hide. The mountains were his best hope and his energy was running low. As he sailed towards them, high up he could see a figure; a girl standing there with her arms outstretched. As he got closer he could see her more clearly. She was of similar age to Sam with dark skin and thick dark curly hair. Furthermore, the earth opening up in front of the troops was not by chance, it was her, she was controlling the earth and bending it to her will, just like Sam was doing with the wind. The girl then dropped her hands and stopped controlling the earth as the troops had stopped their pursuit. This was clearly her aim and her job was done. As she finished she cupped her hands to protect her eyes and looked up into the sky towards Sam. She had seen him and was now waving in his direction. Sam hoped that she was safe. Quite clearly, she possessed great power and was very capable in using it. As she continued to wave at him, Sam flew towards her and landed near. He did not know what to say and stared at her in a bemused fashion. Realising that Sam had nothing to say, the girl began to talk.

"Hi I'm Marta and I think I may have been waiting for you."

Chapter Eleven

The Meeting

Sam approached Marta with some trepidation.

"You have powers." He said.

"Yes I do and so, it would appear, do you. Do you have the annoying voice that talks to you, tells you what to do and is an all-round nuisance?" Marta responded with a smile.

"Yes I do." Sam replied whilst laughing. He was aware that Marta was a friend and at last he was with someone who understood him. "It taught me how to control the wind but you're right it is a nuisance."

"I am here too you know." Responded the voice, aware that they were both mocking him. Not sure that he wanted to be the subject of their joke.

"Good. You are here now and I assume that means you are safe from the armies that were chasing you. It looked like they were a bit upset. Caused them a bit of trouble did you?" Marta asked.

"Yes, I don't think they were too pleased with me." Sam smiled as he replied. He had never had a conversation with a girl similar in age to him. For so long he had only talked to his mother. So, this made a nice change. Especially as she was very attractive too.

"Do you have a name Flyboy? Or should I just call you that?"

Sam was embarrassed for a moment as he realised he hadn't even introduced himself.

"Sorry, Sam. That's my name."

"Sorry Sam is a funny name but it's easy to remember." Marta laughed at her own joke. "Just kidding. Nice to meet you Sam."

"She always thinks she's funny." Interjected the voice.

"We can both hear you." Marta quickly retorted. "So Sam, what's the plan?"

"I need to go back. I need to make sure the people are safe from the troops. Can you help?"

"Of course. Can you get me in there? That way we can force the troops out and create some defences for them."

"I think I can. I've only ever flown alone. So, it will be a first time."

"Oh well, here goes then." Marta put her arms tightly around Sam and readied herself for the experience of flying. She looked at Sam who smiled. He was enjoying Marta holding him tight. "Don't get any ideas fly boy, I'm a spoken for back home, so let's keep this professional."

"Yes boss!" Sam exclaimed. Regardless of what she has just said, he was still very much enjoying himself and her company. He summoned the winds and extended his jacket. He hoped it would create enough resistance to lift them both up. As the winds increased, they carefully lifted up into the air and begin to return to the city.

They landed in the city to see that the inhabitants were beginning to gather. They had gathered together the supplies that Sam had blown around the city, hiding the food but carrying the weapons. They were aware that a revolution was about to begin and there was no time to waste. The troops were also beginning to realise what was happening, having been previously distracted by what Sam had done before and were hastily trying to organise themselves in order to quell the rise of the city inhabitants.

"We need to force them out of the city so that I can build a fortress around it." Marta said to Sam. "If you can bring up the wind I can use the earth to move them back too."

As the troops began to advance Sam controlled the wind and turned it into spiralling hurricanes hurtling towards the armies. As he did this Marta made the earth fly up and into the winds. The armies were being forced back by the sheer velocity and ferociousness of what was confronting them. Not only was the power pushing them backwards but it was impossible to see what they should be aiming for. Furthermore, if they got too close to the winds it was like being brushed with sandpaper. Step by step the armies were being forced back until it became clear that they were fighting against a force greater than themselves. Man by man they began to abandon their orders and began to think of their own survival. Just getting out of the city was becoming a priority. Quickly, most began to flee. This was much more than they had bargained for and retribution was not likely to come from any commanding officer as they were thinking of their own survival too. The battering was merciless. No one would wish to continue. More and more troops fell back and fled and their numbers decreased rapidly. The city inhabitants looked on in amazement at these two young people, finally delivering the freedom that they had craved for so long. The armies were nearly all gone and Sam and Marta strode confidently through the city streets blasting out any small pockets of troops that remained. Despite having only just met they, had already created a formidable team.

Eventually, all the troops had left the city. Sam and Marta stopped using their powers to attack. Sam then flew high into the sky to survey the area and make sure the enemy was long gone. When he had done this he returned to Marta and to a volume of cheers from all that had witnessed the events of the day. As the celebrations began Sam threw his arms around Marta and embraced her with all he could muster, so great was his excitement at what had just happened. Marta eased her way out of Sam's embrace. Whilst the contact was enjoyable, she was aware that there was still much to do.

"Easy fly boy, we are not done yet. Time for me to make this place safe. Oh, and if we are going to spending a lot of time together, a wash is something you need to consider." Marta smiled at Sam as she spoke, wanting to keep everything light between them. She realised that this was likely to be just the beginning of what they had to achieve, and they were going to have to get used to each other's company and not get over excited by every achievement. Sam smiled back at Marta, slightly embarrassed, as washing was not something that he was used to.

Marta then began to do what she had done in so many places, which was to create a safe sealed home for everyone to live in. Everyone looked on in amazement as, once more, Marta began to manipulate the earth to her will. She made the earth rise around the edges of the city to create a fortress to protect everyone and when that was done, she began to make the earth beneath their feet fertile and green. The once dried up city lakes began to fill with water drawn up from the earth below. Bit by bit she created an oasis for them to live in, safe and well. As she finished what she was doing she looked over at Sam who was, like everyone, frozen in amazement.

"Yeah, I can do some stuff." She laughed.

"That was amazing!" Sam screamed. "We are safe now. We can live out our days in peace. Thank you."

"Ah, I think you might need to think about what you just said. Yep, everyone here can have a great life now but that doesn't include you and me. There are still a lot of places around the world that need our help. We were given our powers for a reason and it wasn't to just sit around and taken it easy. Trust me I know, this isn't my first time. So I suggest you find what family you have here and enjoy the party tonight, because it's going to be your farewell tomorrow. Sorry."

Sam paused for a moment as he took in Marta's words.

"That's ok, I kind of thought that might be the case. I just hoped it wouldn't be. I had better find my mum. She's going to like you." Sam then proceeded to walk to the tower where he and his mother lived. As he approached his home he prepared himself to fly up to the top but there was no need. His mother stood at the bottom of the tower out in the street. She had read the letter that he had left and then watched the day's events unfold, from the apartment, as her son became a hero to the entire city. Once it was safe she had made her way down to find him and join in the celebrations that were happening in the streets. As they saw each other they ran towards each other and embraced. So happy to see that they remained unharmed. Marta watched, could not help being reminded of the loved ones that she had left behind. As she let the emotions get to her, a tear came to her eye and the earth beneath her feet began to tremble slightly in sympathy for her, such was her strong connection to it now.

Sam and his mother were distracted by the slight tremor and at once were reminded of Marta's presence.

"Mum, this is Marta and as you might have seen she can do some pretty special things."

"I did." Lucy replied. "But something tells me that you were not here by chance and there is more to do."

"Yes ma'am. But we don't need to discuss that now. I will leave you two alone. I've got some things to sort out and we can chat later." Marta began to walk away realising that Sam would need some time with his mother. That time would be precious as it could be their last, not knowing what the future may be. As she continued to walk further away she began to talk to the voice.

"So what's next? Is he the only one or are there others?"

"There are others that you must find." Replied the voice.

"Yeah I thought as much. So I suppose I give Sam time to say his goodbyes and then head off?"

"Yes."

"Cool. Well at least we might get there quicker now, with him flying us there. In fact I've been travelling round a lot, couldn't you have got him to pick me up sooner?"

"It does not work like that. It is just when the time is right. The next one may be harder. I cannot communicate with him as well as you."

"Great, it's never easy is it? What does this one do?"

"He is fire."

"Ok I'm starting to get it now. Anyway it can all wait till the morning. Right now it looks like a party is about to start and I'm going to be in the middle of it. So no talking to me, you're not going to like my response if you do."

Marta set off to join the crowds that were beginning to gather and celebrate. She was likely to be the guest of honour and was going to enjoy it. The rest of the world could wait for one night and Sam could enjoy the time with his mother too. Let the partying commence.

Chapter Twelve

The Morning After - Part One

A fresh new dawn but Marta was feeling anything but fresh. The blazing sun that shone down on the revived city, brought everything to renewed life and also awoke Marta. But she did not feel revived and alive. She was feeling the effects of partying too hard as the guest of honour, at the city's celebration of freedom. As she awoke, on an abandoned sofa in the middle of the street, she tried to clear her head and remember the night before. As quickly as she remembered she tried to forget; realising that she may have partied too hard and made a bit of a fool of herself. She certainly needed to clean herself up and decided to head to one of the replenished city lakes. As she wandered through the city, she enjoyed watching the inhabitants beginning to put their lives back in order. No longer would they have to wake to the fear of forced labour in service of the troops. Their toil and endeavour would solely be for themselves and their loved ones. Everyone smiled at her as she passed through and there were many offers of food and drink. She took enough for herself but not too much. She was aware that this was just the beginning and it would take a while before there was enough for everyone to eat substantially. For the meantime there are supplies from the abandoned troops quarters to get them by.

As she approached the lake, she realised that she was not the first to have the idea of freshening up there. In the middle of the fresh, clean waters was Sam. He had obviously taken note of what Marta had said and decided to clean himself up.

"Well, well young man, did someone decide to take my advice and clean themselves up? I think I should feel honoured that you are making an effort to keep me happy already." Marta cheekily called out.

Sam hadn't noticed her approaching and was caught out by her presence.

"Don't flatter yourself. It's the first time this lake has had water in a long time. So, I thought I would get in early before anyone else does."

"Of course flyboy you keep telling yourself that. I won't tell. Do you need me to scrub behind your ears? I have got to make sure you are nice and clean for our travels and we don't want your mother to think that I won't look after you."

"Hang on! You're not coming in are you?"

"Of course. What did you think I was going to do?" Marta replied.

"Well it's just that I washed my clothes and hung them up over there, see." Sam gesticulated to a tree nearby, with his head. All this time he had kept his body submerged beneath the water. It was then that Marta realised why.

"Sam! Are you completely naked in there? Who'd have thought you would be so adventurous?" Instantly Marta kicked off her shoes and jumped into the water heading towards Sam.

"Marta! What are you doing?" Sam shrieked as Marta approached. He was becoming more nervous the closer she got, whilst Marta was relishing this moment and decided to make him as uncomfortable as possible.

"Well, it seems like you have come up with a good idea. First I shall swim about a bit and get my clothes clean. Then I suppose I should take them off and get the rest of me clean."

Marta swam right up to Sam and stopped in front of him. Piece by piece she removed her clothing and rinsed them around in the water, showing each item to Sam as she removed them. As each item was came off he become more and more uncomfortable and Marta became more animated and excitable. Sam covered himself with his hands and didn't know where to look. Marta was under the water but Sam could still see enough of this beautiful young girl, through the clear and fresh lake. Thankfully, the water was cold enough to stop him becoming too excited by what he saw but this was his first experience of anything like this. Marta began to speak.

"I know I am teasing you a bit but we are going to be spending a lot of time together from now on. We are going to be eating, drinking, sleeping and even bathing together whenever we get the chance to. So, we might as well get used to each other from the start. So there you go, this is me."

"Ok" Sam nervously replied.

"Right, I'd better put these clothes somewhere to dry." Marta began to climb out the water in order to place her clothes on a nearby rock. Sam remained transfixed by Marta. "You can look away whilst I am doing this. There is a limit!" Marta shouted to Sam.

"Sorry! Of course, I really am sorry. It's just I never have … And you are so beautiful. I'm sorry"

Marta swims back out him and kisses him on the cheek with a friendly peck.

"Bless you. You are sweet. Now let's have a swim and get ourselves cleaned up."

Sam smiled and relaxed his stance. He began to swim around with Marta and started to get used to the new life he had. Maybe spending time with her would turn out to be the greatest adventure of all.

As they enjoyed themselves in the fresh clear waters there didn't seem to be a care in the world and life was good.

Suddenly the voice called to them loudly and sharply.

"You two need to get a move on! There has been a change and we need to get going!"

The Morning After - Part Two

A fresh new dawn but Lyra is feeling anything but fresh. She laid on the floor of the throne room, in the palace, staring intently as the sun broke through the window, following its path around the room as the minutes passed. Everyone was in attendance, except for Scorpius and they waited quiet and still. No one dared make a move or utter a sound for fear of upsetting Lyra any further. It was clear that she was distraught and a single movement might disturb her. Such a movement could break what Lyra was indulging in. It may cause her to use her powers without mercy on anyone. How long they might be there no one knew; but they must endure the pain of keeping still and quiet, even if it lasted for hours or days, until she is ready to interact with them. Occasionally, she let out a sigh or a groan but not one of pain, more of someone debating with herself. Sometimes agreeing, sometimes not but it was clear that there was an internal argument within Lyra.

So, they waited; moment by moment, minute by minute, hour by hour. As they waited, some leaned on each other for support. So long had they been standing that their legs are beginning to tire and give in. But they must not give in, they must not fall to the floor, they must not show weakness, for if they did, things would surely be over for them.

Eventually relief, the signal came that Scorpius was about to arrive. As he swept into the room everyone began to lower themselves to show respect for their leader. This also gave them the chance to move and recover themselves slightly. They began to move towards him to begin the days' business but are waved away as the only concern Scorpius had was for his daughter laying on the floor in distress. He moved down the stairs of the elevated throne towards Lyra and began to speak.

"What troubles you Lyra? Why are you so down? Surely I can help your mood, my daughter."

Scorpius showed some trepidation in his approach. He had dealt with Lyra being in bad moods throughout her childhood but this was clearly different.

"Failure Daddy, that's what has made me so sad. Failure and weakness." Lyra responded.

"My dear, our troops have had some setbacks but we shall win in the end. The fools that resist shall soon learn that their efforts are worthless. Soon they will be begging for our mercy. Do not worry my dear daughter. We will prevail."

"It is not the troops that have failed. It is not the troops that are weak." Lyra began to rise. "It is their leadership that is weak. They were defeated by those that have powers and if I do not act, they will be defeated again. I can no longer restrain myself from using all that I have. There are others and if I do not seek to gain control of them, we will be defeated for all time. We can afford to lose the odd battle but not the war."

"My dear daughter, I think you are being too hard on yourself. The armies will carry out your orders as you wish. They have been very loyal to me for so long, they will do as commanded by you, for you speak on behalf of their leader, Scorpius."

"Indeed, I speak on behalf of the weak."

"Excuse me!" Scorpius was shocked by Lyra's response.

"The armies see powers against them, when they fight, too great for them and they are afraid. They run and hide. Why? Because there is nothing to fear if they do so. Is their leader as powerful? Should they be fearful for running away? No, because their leader does not have such powers. But I do. It is time for all to be as fearful of failing! That way they will give their all without question. You are weak Daddy dearest and it is time for you to go."

"But Lyra!"

"Speak no more." With a turn of her hand directed at Scorpius she immediately takes away his ability to speak. With the closing of her hand she has pulled his voice from him and crushed it in her palm. All are aware that she is unleashing the full use of her powers. Many had suspected that her Father had restrained her from using them fully, and now they were beginning to see that was true and they should be very afraid. Scorpius fumbled around and moved away from Lyra, unable to communicate to anyone who might help him. He climbed up the stairs, towards his throne, seeking protection. But the closer he got to anyone, the more they moved away. Lyra was scanning the room to see the reaction from everyone gathered. They are aware that control was changing right before their eyes and they are not going to interfere. They were making themselves ready to swap their allegiance the moment it arrived. That moment appeared to be now.

Scorpius managed to reach the top of the stairs by his throne. It was almost as though he believed that if he was physically higher than Lyra, some of his status might return. She was aware of this and chose to display her powers further. In an instant she flew from where she was to the top of stairs and knocked her father to the floor as she landed. She began to speak as all looked on in amazement.

"You see! You are weak and powerless. You can do nothing against me or those that would choose to rise against us. You are a failure, just like when you failed to save my Mother."

Again, with a sharp movement of her hand, the weapons held by the guards flew from their hands or sheaths and headed towards Scorpius. No screams could be heard coming from Scorpius as he had no voice but the physical actions were clear. The fear and terror of a man witnessing an array of weapons hurtling towards him. Then they stopped! Just inches away from doing him harm. They hung motionless in the air, forcing Scorpius to remain still on the floor. One move and they would pierce him.

Lyra circled him and relished the moment. The change of power was clear to see. As she looked around the room everyone began to lower themselves down in deference to the new leader.

"Take him away and lock him up! He will no longer be spoken of. It is time for us to move on, to defeat those that stand against us. Let me be clear. We are fighting against those that have power and there are others to come. But do not be afraid, they are controlled by one very much like me. They seek to tip the balance of power. But I am the greatest of them all and I assure you the scales will weigh heavily on our side. Even now I have sought out the others and have blocked the communication to them. Balance is already being restored in our favour. Ready yourselves, because we shall be victorious."

Chapter Thirteen

The Time is Now

Marta and Sam had quickly swum back to the banks of the lake and put on their damp clothes. The voice sounded distressed and they clearly needed to get a move on. There was a problem and they needed to find out why the voice was suddenly in a panic.

"Ok, so what's the panic?" Marta asked. "Is it so bad that you couldn't have let us have a bit of fun for a few minutes?"

"Indeed it is." Replied the voice. "The forces that we fight against have just become stronger and we are already under attack without it being seen."

"Hang on, we just gave the armies a bit of a bashing, surely they should be getting a bit weaker. Scorpius should be starting to get a bit worried by now."

"Scorpius is no longer in charge. He has been overthrown."

"Is that not a good thing?" Marta replied. Sam nodded in agreement.

"Lyra is now in charge."

"Isn't she his bonkers daughter?" Sam interjected.

"Not at all. She is very powerful. I once used to communicate with her until she cast me away."

"Wow! You mean to tell me that someone actually managed to get rid of you. Now that is a person I want to meet." Marta joked.

"She is definitely someone you do not wish to meet any time soon. She is reaching the peak of her powers and is taking control. My bond with you two has grown strong and it is easy for us to talk but she is blocking my communication with others. If we don't get to them soon we may lose our chance to find them and join together. If we fail all will be lost. One may already have been captured, as I cannot locate him."

"So how are we going to find him then? I assume if we don't then your masterplan, whatever it is, doesn't work."

"You must travel east to where I knew he was, then try to track him from there. I will guide you."

"Ok Sam, it's time to say your goodbyes. It's horrible I know but I've done it before so at least I can sympathise with you." Marta realised that this would be tough for him. She was doing her best to be sympathetic but also that there was no option for either of them other than to start on their travels.

"It's ok. I knew this was coming. Just give me time to pack a few things and see my mum." Sam replied.

With that Sam set off to get ready.

"This is not going to be easy for him. At least when I left my home we were not so aware of the danger. It sounds a lot worse now and we are just asking him to leave his home and put his life in danger. This place has just become safe. It is certainly hard to leave."

"If you don't carry on, this place will not be safe for long. Lyra will be looking for you. So, staying in one place is not an option. From now on, wherever you are will be in danger. There are too many innocent people here to put at risk." The voice responded.

"Oh well, there goes my summer of chilling by the lake. It's never a party with you is it? Well presumably the quickest way to travel is if we fly, but we won't get far if we have to just cling on to each other all the time. We had better build something that can carry both of us up high where no one can see us." With that Marta set about building a glider of sorts.

She enlisted the help of the city inhabitants and they scavenged together the necessary parts. With that they managed to build a glider. Light enough to fly but strong enough to hold them. They put together a wooden structure that could be folded away when required. They would surely have to hide at times, so it needed to be able to fold up. Over the frame, they stretched fabric taken from the abandoned troop tents. Marta hoped it would be strong enough to hold them but they would never know for certain until they were flying. It was a risk that they were going to have to take. Underneath the wing structure, they fashioned a frame and a net that would hold her, Sam and enough supplies to keep them going for a while. Time was valuable. So, the less they wasted trying to procure things, the better. Hopefully, it would all work as expected but time was a luxury that they could not afford. Any adaptations would have to done on the road as they used the glider and worked out its faults.

Whilst Marta attended to getting ready for departure, Sam spent his remaining time with his Mother, Lucy. Unlike Marta, Sam only had the one parent and was deeply concerned about leaving her on her own. They had spent so much time hidden up in the tower, just the two of them, that she did not know anyone that lived in the city. Sam was concerned that she would be lonely, as well as finding it hard to survive. But he hadn't factored in that he was now a hero in the city and the inhabitants were only too willing to meet and offer help to the man who had saved them. He introduced his mother to all they met and asked them all to take care of her whilst he continued to take the fight to the enemy. They all agreed without hesitation. There was one family that Sam wished his Mother to meet and he returned to the shop where he had returned the lost girl.

The moment they saw Sam they rushed towards him, realising that they had already known the city's hero. They wanted to show their gratitude that they would no longer have to hide away, in cramped quarters, struggling to survive. They were aware that there would be tough times ahead until the city's inhabitants got themselves organised but hope of a brighter future was fuel enough for life right now.

"This is my mother, Lucy. She will be alone now as I have to leave. I was wondering if you could look after her until I return."

"Of course." Replied the mother he had met previously. "She will be part of our family now and we will look after and safeguard her, just as you have us."

Lucy was ushered into the shop and immediately began to settle in with the family. As there wasn't the need to hide away, they had already began to extend their living area to surrounding buildings and had scavenged enough already, to make themselves a bit more comfortable. Lucy should be fine as part of this community and Sam felt more at ease. Although his destiny was to leave and sacrifice his time with the only family had, he realised it was much better to be involved in trying to create a new world in which there was a chance of a much healthier existence. At least there may be an opportunity to have a longer lasting life with more time to cherish special moments and maybe one day have a larger family of his own making.

After a bit of time with them Sam realised he needed to leave and begin his journey with Marta.

He hugged Lucy goodbye and managed to prise himself away from her. There is surely nothing much stronger than a mother's will to hold on to her child and never let them go but eventually Sam managed to free himself and walk away. He glanced back only once to take a final look at his tearful mother and then strode on, resolute.

He came upon Marta who was finishing the glider with the help of some inhabitants. She had also gathered enough supplies to keep them going for a while. Marta realised that during their travels she would mainly be a passenger and her task would be to look after Sam and keep him fit enough to sustain the flying required. She had gathered together food, clothing and bedding. This would keep them going for a while and would mean that they could rest in safe, out of the way places and not venture too close to danger. They loaded it all up in the net below the glider, which would be tight but still enough room for the both of them with everything they were carrying.

"You've done an amazing job with this Marta."

"Thanks. It's nothing fancy but hopefully it will do the job. Do you think you can make it work?"

"Well let's give it a try and maybe adjust it if we need to."

So Sam and Marta loaded themselves onto the glider and began to try it out. Sam was cautious at first, not wanting to put Marta at risk. He summoned the winds to lift the glider off the ground. Gently at first, only raising it a few metres from the ground. Lifting it up wasn't a problem but getting the balance right was the key to their safety. There was no use gaining height, only to spiral out of control. After a few attempts and making some adjustments they were soon ready to depart.

"Are you ready?" Sam asked Marta. "We are going to have to go very high to avoid detection, so it may be a bit scary."

"It's ok, I trust you." Marta smiled at him to put him at ease. Although, she was a bit scared at the thought of flying so high, in a hastily put together glider, she did indeed trust Sam. They hadn't known each other for long but a bond had formed between them. Marta was confident that Sam would do his best to look after her, just as she would look after him. So without hesitation she climbed aboard ready for departure.

Sam climbed aboard too and concentrated on controlling his powers; summoning the wind, lifting them off the ground and high into the air. As they climbed, they could see the inhabitants waving up at them, becoming smaller every moment. When they reached a distance that was out of sight, Sam began to move them along in flight. The more confident he became the faster they went and the more distance they travelled.

"I shall guide you on your journey. Listen to me and you shall reach where you need to be." Said the voice. And so they did, as they began their quest for others like them.

Chapter Fourteen

Fire

No date, No time, No location

Somewhere in the Far East a large troop of soldiers marched endlessly on, travelling great distances in order to return home. They had not had a hot meal in some time now. They had supplies but are unable to heat them up. They could make fire; they could feed themselves a hot meal if they desired but they were too afraid to do so. They had a job to do and nothing must stop them from achieving their task. Day by day, night by night they marched. On occasion they stopped briefly, feeding on cold food and water. They never set up camp, just slept enough to once again begin their journey. They were loyal and faithful. They were in service to their new leader, the almighty and powerful Lyra. Failure was not an option. They were driven on day by day, by the fear of failure. Not only were they afraid of their new leader but the cargo they carried also filled them with dread. They are aware that they need to deliver it to Lyra or they faced extinction from her or destruction from what they were transporting. Sacrifice was the only option. Ignore the pain, the hunger, the exhaustion, complete the task, deliver the cargo and reward would surely be theirs.

So, they carried on relentlessly, through all climates and all landscapes, pulling with them a cart. Within that cart was a large box made of metal, surrounded by armed soldiers. Some carried weapons, some carried water. They needed to achieve their goal. The metal box had a few holes; enough for what it contained to breathe and to be fed. But it must never be released until it reached its destination. It was far too dangerous for the troops to deal with. Only the power of Lyra could control what was within. For in the box contained a young man with powers.

The young man in question was Nikki. Most people held within a metal box would be afraid, fearful of what their future held but not Nikki. He was aware that those outside of his restrained confinement were terrified of him and that waiting for the right time and moment, was all he needed. He was used to this situation, as most people had been afraid of him all his life. Nikki had the power to control fire.

He had grown up in the Far Eastern regions of this cruel harsh world. His features were representative of this, only with a slightly more scorched appearance from his continual dalliance with fire. As he had grown up he became aware of his powers when he was drawn into a fire. He was drawn in by the amazing beauty that the dancing flames created. But rather than being engulfed and burnt by the flames he was suddenly dancing with them like a couple in perfect synchronisation. They did not burn him or even touch his flesh. They just warmed him and filled him with energy and power. Over time, he taught himself to control the flames and use them to his advantage. Although, he could not create fire himself, it certainly obeyed him as though he was its Master. However, the better he became at controlling fire the more his own people became afraid of him. They started to see him as a monster, as a demon. It was not natural for someone to be able to do this and being around him would surely put them in danger. Even his own family could not hide their fear, assuming that he had become possessed by something evil. As time passed, everyone kept their distance and Nikki became unloved and alone. Eventually, he stopped trying to seek affection from anyone and sought out solace for himself. If no one wanted to love him then why try to be loved. He was capable of great things on his own. By now all he needed was a spark to obtain fire, so had all he needed to look after himself. He left the people he knew, his family and friends that had once loved him but did not anymore and sought out a place to live on his own. All he took was a couple of knives with him, sharp enough to cause damage with their original purpose, but when scraped together they were enough to create the sparks for fire. That's all Nikki needed to survive. To fight, to cook, to keep himself warm. Nothing else, especially not love. Being alone and hidden from the world suited him. It was after all, better than being rejected by everyone.

A metal box was nothing, not even used as a prison. Nikki might bemoan that he hadn't been paying attention but he was not bothered. Clearly the troops had been watching him from a distance whilst he had been living his solitary existence but he had not noticed or cared. He did not care that they had taken him while he slept and encased him within the box, because in fact Nikki was enjoying every moment of it. He was enjoying hearing the voices and activity outside. For so long he had been alone, it was some time since he had heard conversation and it kept him amused. He was revelling in the fact that despite him doing nothing and being contained, they were still so afraid of him. So afraid that they dare not light a fire and heat food or water, for fear that he may be able to control it and burn them to a cinder. How wonderful that he had that much power without doing a thing. How wonderful that someone wanted to see him so much that they had gone to all this trouble, despite the fact that the person at the other end was Lyra. Nikki was definitely not afraid or distressed, he was happy. He could probably escape from the box but if there was a spark to make fire he might choke through lack of oxygen within his confined space. So, it wasn't worth the effort. He decided to just relax and enjoy the ride.

Hour by hour, day by day, the troops carried on travelling to their destination. No one knew how much further they had to travel or how long it would take. The more exhausted they became the longer it took; no longer certain of where they were on their journey.

No date, no time, no location.

The weather now, seemed permanently against them. Every step they took was made harder by pushing against the harsh winds that seemed to blow directly at them, chilling them to bone. Every hill seemed to get steeper and harder to climb as they travelled. Hour by hour, day by day, never ending pain and harsh toil against the elements. Every man was beginning to break, only driven on by the fear of failure. Yet more winds, yet more hills, trudging through the mud that surrounded their weary legs.

At a certain point, whilst climbing yet another steep and unforgiving hill, the commander turned and looked back at his exhausted troops behind him. He was aware that all of them were at the point of breaking. In order for them to continue he would have to let them rest for a while. If they went much further in this state, they would surely all break and give up. He ordered them to stop and take a break. They fed themselves, what they could and then began to huddle together for warmth. The commander realised that he had to break the routine and allow them a longer recovery time. All needed sleep and they would have to rotate who stayed awake and stood guard, whilst the others rested. They arranged who would stand guard and the rest then huddled together in piles and began to get sleep. At last a break, at last some relief. Or so they thought. As they huddled together seeking warmth from each other, the weather got stronger and fiercer, the winds penetrating every small gap between them, taking away any chance of being comfortable and warm. Then as the winds increased more and more, the earth kicked up at them, battering them relentlessly with pellets of stones and mud. The troops tried to cover and protect themselves from the constant onslaught of the weather but the more they tried to shield themselves the worse it got. Moment by moment the winds got stronger and the objects hitting them got larger.

Then the moment of realisation hit and spread through all the troops. They were not just unlucky and had chosen to rest at the wrong time. They had been caught in a trap. This was no coincidence. They were under attack.

Chapter Fifteen

Teamwork

Marta and Sam had travelled for some time. They had managed to travel great distances with their glider. To begin with they travelled in short bursts as Sam wasn't able to maintain flight for very long. At first it would only be an hour, maybe two, before they would have to set down and rest. Each time Marta would tend to their needs and let Sam recover, as he would go until he was completely exhausted. She would make sure that they were well sheltered, then they would eat and sleep. As the days passed Sam's powers grew stronger and he was able to maintain flight for longer. He found it easier to balance the glider, which made it less effort. As the days passed they were able to maintain flight for hours at a time, allowing them to cover vast areas and search for others like them.

Trying to find what they were looking for was not as easy as they had planned. Lyra was now blocking communication between the voice and those that they sought. On many occasions they had stopped, thinking that they had made a discovery and found someone with powers, only to be disappointed. Too many communities were being tricked by people who they believed had special powers but mostly they were being deceived by parlour tricks that were no more than misdirection. Day by endless day, they continued their search until they stumbled on a village in the Far East, that spoke of a young man that used to live with them but was forced to live alone because of his control over fire. They told how the troops had come and taken him away. Marta and Sam at last knew that they were on the right track and had found a trail that they could follow.

They were a long way behind the troops but at least now it would not take them long to catch up using the glider. After a couple of days of searching they found them. A large troop, marching towards their homeland, pulling a cart with a large metal box. They were certain that this was what they were looking for. The next thing was to create their plan of attack.

This was a large troop. Much bigger than what they had encountered before and so they decided that they would need to be much smarter than before. A direct attack in an open space might leave them more vulnerable. This was a powerful looking troop of soldiers and Marta and Sam were still very new in the art of warfare. They were not certain that their powers would last long enough to combat such a force whilst they were so strong. Time was to be their weapon. The longer they had to endure harsh conditions, the weaker the troops would become. So Marta and Sam made their plan and stuck to it. With all the time they had spent together their bond had become stronger and they were forming a good team.

So day by day they kept out of sight but began to wear down the troops. As the army marched relentlessly on, towards their destination, Sam directed the winds straight at them. Every day they would march directly into them, no matter which way they were travelling. The troops regularly changed direction but they were always being battered by the wind. Marta changed the ground beneath their feet, always making it uneven and difficult to maintain balance on or thick with mud, so that every step would sap the strength from their limbs. Each hill or mountain, that they tried to climb, would become steeper and more unforgiving as they tried to push on and complete their task. Slowly but relentlessly Marta and Sam drained the soldiers of every last bit of energy they had. Each day the troops became weaker and weaker, barely able to put one foot in front of the other but still going on, afraid of failure. Each time the troops took a break so did Sam and Marta, restoring the energy they required. Occasionally only one of them would use their powers on the soldiers whilst the other took an opportunity to rest. But the plan was working. As they stayed out of sight they could see that the armies were breaking down, getting weaker and less motivated with each step. It was only a matter of time before they could attack and finish the job.

The moment arrived after a long stretch of wearing them down, when they decided to stop halfway up a hill. They were broken and the commander stopped for rest. As they laid down their weapons and huddled together for warmth, now was the time to attack.

Sam increased the winds to chill every man to the bone and as they huddled tighter together to protect themselves, they became an easy target. Marta sent up the earth into the wind and began to batter them with pellets of mud and stone. The soldiers then knew that this was not a chance happening. They were under attack. However, the commander was at a loss as to who they should fight against, because they could not see anyone to fight. Marta and Sam were still quite a distance away, as their powers did not require them to be too close. As for the troops, they could barely keep their eyes open as the wind and dirt was blinding them. Moment by moment Sam increased the winds and Marta increased the size of the stones battering at the army. They were helpless against the onslaught and the realisation was that all was lost. It was time to escape before they were hurt any more. Even if they had been able to see their enemy, they had no energy left for a fight. So they ran, back down the hill and away from anything or anyone that might do them harm. The commander tried to encourage them back and to secure the package that they were to deliver. But all was lost. As a few faithful troops tried to recover the cart with the metal box, Marta pulled up the earth from beneath them and turned the cart over. As it did so the metal box crashed to the floor and sprung open. Nikki was now free.

Nikki was cautious as he climbed out of the box. From inside, he had heard all the commotion and was aware that he was now in the middle of an attack. Although, he had been captured by the troops, he was still not aware whose side he should be on, as he found himself in the middle of the battle that was happening around him. He could not see who the troops were fighting against but they must be very dangerous to cause this much chaotic fear. Nikki looked around and saw on the ground the two knives that he usually carried around. They must have been loaded onto the cart when he was captured and had now fallen to the floor along with him and the metal box. He picked them up, one in each hand and scraped them together, just as a butcher might when he sharpens his tools before slicing open the flesh of a beast. The knives began to spark and gave Nikki what he needed to call upon his power. From the smallest spark, Nikki could feel the energy charging through him as he became connected to it. It surged through him and he felt it in every part of his body. It was euphoric and glorious all at once. In an instant the spark became a flame and then a sword of fire stemming out from each knife. He was once again in control of his own destiny and he stood there rooted to the ground like a fearsome warrior scanning all around him and assessing the situation, before deciding who to attack.

The remaining troops had witnessed this and realised that the worst case scenario was upon them. Not only were they under attack from an unseen force but the prisoner that they feared so much was now on the loose and could seek revenge on them. They were lost as to which way to go. Wherever they ran it would be dangerous. Run towards the onslaught of the attack on them, run towards the man standing by them with swords of fire or run away and face the inevitable revenge of Lyra after they had failed. Hopeless and abandoned by the others that had already fled they were faced with an impossible situation.

Nikki revelled in seeing the fear in their eyes as he realised that his mere presence was enough to take control of the situation. He did not move from the spot that he was rooted to, instead he just turned his head towards any soldier around him, stared directly at them and smiled with the knowledge that at any moment he could strike them down. Each soldier, that caught his eye, immediately turned and fled. The decision was easy, survive today, run from the danger in front of them and hope that they may make amends for it in the future and not incur the wrath of Lyra.

One by one they fled, as Nikki started to move towards them with the demonic smile on his face, until there were none left and he was alone on the hillside. He stood majestically as he surveyed all around him and as he did so the winds began to die down. Nikki then realised that not everybody had gone, because there was a young woman confidently striding towards him with a smile on her face. As she approached he realised that she was not at all afraid by the fact that he was brandishing two swords of fire. She began to speak.

"Hiya Smokey, I'm Marta. You can put the fire sword thing you've got going on there away, I'm a friend."

"Why should I believe or trust you? What's to stop me from just striking you down right here and now?"

"Ok, good point, I was hoping we weren't going to have to play these games." Instantly Sam swept down from on high blasting Nikki and extinguishing his flames, whilst Marta covered his hands and knives with mud drawn up from the ground. Nikki stood there as he realised that he was not the only one with powers and he was also outnumbered.

"Now you may think that we aren't being friendly but I could have buried you in the ground up to your neck, or Sam could have lifted you into the air and dropped you in a lake, so we are really." Marta joked with a huge grin on her face.

"Before you ask, yes she is always like this." Sam quipped.

"Well someone has to keep you in order, and now it appears I have Mister Smokey and moody to deal with too."

Nikki was understandably still cross at what had just happened but was aware that he may just have to stand there and listen.

"So, we have come here for you. As you might have noticed we have powers too and we hoped that you might want to join up with us. The world has been a pretty rubbish place for quite some time and if we team up, there is quite a lot we can do to sort out this mess. What do you think?"

Nikki stood for a moment pondering what Marta had just said. He was quite clearly outnumbered by those with powers, so trying to fight was out of the question. Also, he had spent a long time being alone and standing in front of him were two people who actually wanted to be around him. They were not afraid of him or had any desire to cage him up. In fact they had just made an effort to set him free, so maybe it might be worth giving them a chance. As he stood there thinking about his options Marta began to speak again.

"Well his face has gone from angry to confused. So, we might get a response soon. You never know."

"Maybe he is considering what life would be like with you. Perhaps being shut in a box might be a better option." Sam laughed at his own comment whilst Marta flashed him a look of I will get you later. A smirk also came across Nikki's face as he began to enjoy the banter and he decided to take Sam's side.

"So part of what I have to do is put up with her all the time. Sounds tough." Nikki joked.

"Yeah. The voice said I would have to make some sacrifices for the greater good. So I suppose hanging out with Marta was what he was talking about. I'm Sam by the way." Sam was enjoying this. He began to realise that if another joined them Marta may not be so bossy with him all the time, as she would have someone else to keep an eye on. She on the other hand was not quite so amused at the thought of two of them having exchanges like this and thought she had better take control of the situation again.

"So, enough of the chat about me. Shall we actually get back to the business in hand? As you now know my name is Marta and we have been sent here by the voice to rescue you and continue on our journey in order to find others like us and help all that we can. So, two questions. Are you in and what's your name?"

"I'm Nikki. The voice?" Nikki responded.

"Yeah you know the one. Really annoying. Always coming up with ways to make life more difficult." Marta replied.

"Yet again I need to remind you that I am always here." Responded the voice to Marta's usual critical and joking response.

"Wow, I haven't heard that in a while." Nikki replied slightly in shock at hearing the voice. "It disappeared a long time ago. I kept hearing others as well until I managed to block them all out."

"Probably not best to mention that you heard lots of voices. Sounds a bit crazy if you ask me. But hey, good job blocking it out. Maybe one day you can teach me that. The peace and quiet would be lovely. Although I would still have to put up with Sam." Marta couldn't resist taking a little swipe back at Sam. She wouldn't want him thinking that she wasn't going to control his every move still.

"Hey, I'm not that bad." Sam protested.

"No but without me keeping you out of trouble who knows where you'd be." Marta smiled at Sam realising that she was once again asserting her control over him. The voice then cut in.

"I'm afraid that Lyra has probably blocked my communication with Nikki. She grows stronger all the time."

"So you are telling me she can match up to you! That's not what we want to hear."

"As I have said before, it's all about balance. She will be able to match me in many ways. That is why we must join together and create a strong force. In time all will become clear in how we must proceed. For now we must continue on and find the last one. She will be expecting us but it is a long journey."

"Excellent! Sounds like we have another girl on the horizon. But we haven't yet discovered if Smokey boy here is going to happily come along for the ride, or is he going back in the box?" Marta and Sam looked at Nikki awaiting his decision. He stared back at them, sizing up his options before he replied.

"So, she constantly talks and bosses everyone around and now I hear that voice again. It's not looking too appealing. But I feel sorry for this Sam guy, he looks like he might need some company if not protection from you, so I think I will tag along and see where this goes." Nikki smiled at Marta as he said this, making it quite clear that he wasn't going to be a pushover like Sam.

"Great! Not exactly the response that I was hoping for but the end result is right. Well we have the power of fire along with the abilities to control the wind and the earth, so I assume the girl we are looking for can control water."

"Indeed." Replied the voice. "You will need to travel overseas and it is too far for Sam to carry you all. Head for the coast and find a boat with which to travel."

"Ok." Responded Marta. She then looked at the boys. "Well you two heard the voice, let's get a move on. The sooner we find her the better."

The boys then began to move up to the top of the hill where Sam and Marta had hidden their belongings before the attack. Marta looked on whilst Sam was chatting excitedly with Nikki. He was obviously happy to have some new company. Marta was pleased for him, as she had formed a strong bond with him and cared for him deeply. Whether she'd create the same bond with Nikki wasn't so clear. Only time would tell.

She caught up with them and listened to Sam talk about their adventures prior to meeting Nikki. As he continued with his story telling they began to relax and enjoy themselves before embarking on the next stage of their journey.

Chapter Sixteen

The Mercy of Lyra

In the throne room, of the palace, rows of soldiers knelt before Lyra, heads bowed showing their remorse for failing their leader. They are afraid. They were sent to achieve a certain task for her and they had failed. They had been defeated in battle by those with forces beyond their understanding and had considered never returning but for many this was their home. They had struggled with the thought of never seeing their loved ones ever again and after much debate between them they had decided that they would have to risk the wrath of Lyra or forever be cast out and away from their families. Those in the lower ranks felt sure that their commanders would take most of the blame and they would be likely go unpunished. It was a risk worth taking.

As Lyra sat on her throne, pondering her decision; many were shaking through fear, starvation and exhaustion. They had given everything to try and achieve their task, only to be left in this difficult situation. All hoped for some kind of mercy from Lyra but they did not really expect it to happen.

Lyra looked down upon everyone. Her beauty alone would make her intimidating to most but her power added to her magnificence. She appeared to be taking her time at deciding what to do. Perhaps realising that now she had complete control over all matters she needed to make the right decisions in order to rule over her subjects. She was also aware that the wait was building the tension and increasing the focus on her. Eventually, she rose from her throne and began to address all that were assembled.

"I see before me a large troop that are waiting for me to pass judgement on them. They are aware that they failed me and as such kneel, remorseful and humbled before their leader in the hope that I will forgive them. What is their crime? Did they fail to give their all in service to me? No, I don't think they did. I see troops that are starved, exhausted and have tried to give everything in service to me, their leader. Should they be punished for that, I don't think so. Where they have failed is that they were not strong enough to carry out their task. That responsibility lies with their training and how we as a kingdom have previously failed in making sure our troops are ready to face these ordeals. There are going to be many difficult times ahead and we must be ready or we will lose against these new powers that seek to destroy us. So, what should I do with these troops before me? Should I punish them for their efforts? Or should I let them go free to return to their families and forget what happened? The answer is neither. We need to make sure these soldiers have the strength and resolve to fight for us and defend us in the future. I am here to help you. I will make sure that you are stronger and you will fight for your loved ones. Therefore, I am going to be merciful."

There is a buzz around the room. This was not what everyone gathered thought was going to happen. The troops were still kneeling in front of her with their heads bowed. They started to believe that their ordeal might be over. They started to look sideways towards each other with looks of relief that the unthinkable was happening. Lyra continued to speak.

"In order to make you stronger and have the desire to fight, defend and survive, I have devised a way to help you. In a moment you will leave here. You will be taken to a camp that will strengthen your resolve and desire. It will start with six months hard labour. During that time you will be fed only water and the waste from the city. After the six months, if you have survived, you will be re-enlisted into the army and retrained in the hardest extremes imaginable for the next year. I suggest that this will ensure that you have built up enough strength, in that time, to survive anything. So next we will need to build up your resolve, as such will we send you to the outer regions of our kingdom to serve for the next ten years. There you will build up the resolve to survive anything in order that you may return home one day to your loved ones. Anyone who fails to complete this or tries to leave, will be treated as a deserter and will be dealt with accordingly. I think this is a suitable outcome for all of you. Be grateful that I have shown you such mercy. Take them away."

As the soldiers are led out of the room Lyra returned to her throne. Crying and screams could be heard from the soldiers as well as some gathered in Lyra's court. They were aware that they may never see some of the troops again.

"Why such sadness? They lived to fight another day and if not they have given a great sacrifice to us all. We should all be happy."

Those gathered that were affected began to stifle their emotions in order to avoid Lyra's anger.

"Good. Now it is time for us to prepare for the battles to come. These young people, with powers are still raw and they are not yet complete in what they need. They are no match for me. We need to encounter them soon, so I can crush them where they stand. But first we need to recruit and train larger armies. We shall go out into the kingdom, travelling from place to place and I will personally persuade all the inhabitants to join me in this crusade. We shall win and it will be glorious!"

With that Lyra swept out of the room, followed by her commanders and leading politicians. Lyra's idea of persuasion was something that all should fear and no one wanted to be on the wrong side of her now.

Chapter Seventeen

Water

A tropical island in the middle of a vast ocean, barely touched by the damage and chaos in the rest of the world. So far removed from everything and everyone that it has become forgotten by all. The islanders lead a happy life. Food is plentiful and the sun shines on this paradise. The islanders are blessed. Not only that, they have a leader that provides for them, cares for them, loves them.

It was a typical morning on the island and most are gathered at the sea front. They are there to help with the daily, bountiful catch from the ocean. Although the fishermen were great at using their skills, handed down from generation to generation, they were also aided in their endeavours by their beloved leader.

Her name is Namaka. She is young and beautiful. In contrast to most of the others on the island, she is pale with long blond hair and sharp blue eyes. Because of these features, all on the island knew she was special from the moment she was born. They knew right away that they were blessed with someone who would make their lives all that they hoped for. As such, she was always treated with love and reverence. In return she made sure that they were well cared for and protected from the cruel, harsh world away from their home. She did not disappoint, because as she grew older she developed the powers that she used to help all of her people. Namaka could control water and she had used this power well to create an idyllic life for all. So much so, that the islanders were happy to have her as their leader despite the fact that she was barely an adult.

Today was like most others. The fishermen waited in their boats off the coast of the island; not too far out and still in sight of land. They only needed to be in waters deep enough to drop their nets and wait for what was to happen next. When they were ready, the next stage of the daily routine would begin. Namaka would arrive, happily walking through the islanders, talking and embracing whoever wished to do so. She was not a leader that wished to feel separate from her people. In fact, she desired nothing more than to be part of her community, as though they were all family. Her arrival created joy amongst everyone and her popularity was strong. Even the fishermen were waiting for her smile, as they were used to her taking her time and making sure that anyone who wanted to have contact with her was granted that time.

Eventually she reached the waters' edge and the day's rituals and routines could begin. Namaka concentrated on the task at hand and as she did, so the waters began to gather around her and lift her up onto a throne, made entirely from the sea. The throne then carried her out towards the fishermen and as she reached them she began to speak.

"My apologies my friends. I know I am late again. But there was too much joy to be had from talking to everyone. Shall we begin?"

The fishermen acknowledged her apology without much thought. They were happy and were used to her being late. They readied their nets for what was about to happen.

Then in an instant Namaka began to manipulate the sea, moving it in different directions at a whim, being sure not to upset the boats but making the water around them twist and turn in a frenzy of action. By doing so the fish are thrown around and into the waiting nets. One by one the fishermen pulled in the nets and signalled that they had enough. Quickly they then sorted through their catch, making sure that they had not caught anything unnecessary or had too much. They returned what they didn't need to the sea, before any damage could be done. Namaka then directed the waves to push the boats back to the waiting crowds on the beach. As with most days the waiting crowds were cheering and clapping with excitement. They were grateful for every day that they received such a bounty. As they approached the beach, the waiting crowds then guided the boats up onto the land and begin to offload the catch. Each net was opened and sorted. There was no individual ownership of what was caught as it was shared amongst all the islanders; making sure that everyone had enough to eat. Everything was done that way on the island, with all goods that they had and therefore no one went without. It was a simple way of life but it was a happy and healthy one too.

As the sorting continued songs could be heard amongst the lively chatter. The joy was undeniable and there was no desire for a change of lifestyle from the islanders. Then through the hustle and bustle came a shout. First from one of the islanders and then more as they witnessed something they hadn't seen in a very long time. The islanders' attention was drawn towards a small sail boat, on the horizon, heading towards them at speed. Not only had they not seen a boat from outside the island in a long time but this one seemed to be powered by such strong winds that it was travelling faster than any of them had witnessed before.

Everyone looked to Namaka for guidance as they were not quite sure what they were witnessing. She smiled reassuringly at them, as she was not surprised by what she was seeing. In fact, she had been expecting it. She summoned up the sea to create her throne and travelled out to the oncoming boat. As she approached, she could see three dishevelled young people of similar age to herself on board. She pulled up alongside the boat and began to speak.

"Welcome to our island. The voice told me that you were coming. So, I am pleased to see you have got here safely."

Chapter Eighteen

Island Life

Marta and the boys had managed to navigate the ocean and travel to the island where Namaka lived. It had been a long and tough journey. Just travelling to the coast by foot had been difficult enough through arduous terrain but they had to change direction several times to avoid the troops that were on the lookout for them. Eventually, when they arrived at the coast, they had to find a boat capable of the journey. By now most boats had been abandoned from a time long forgotten and most were broken shells of what they once were. Finally, they found one, that with a little repair, they could use. They managed to patch it up using parts from other wrecks left nearby; all the time trying to remain hidden from those who would capture them, given a chance. It wasn't perfect and it wasn't luxurious. It wasn't even as big as they would have liked but it would do. There came a point, whether it was good enough or not, when they would have to set sail. Staying in one place for too long would always be a danger. So, they managed to paddle the boat away from the coast, under the cover of darkness, before the sun rose. When they felt that they had got enough distance between them and the mainland, they raised the sails and relied on Sam to conjure enough wind to move them along at a fast pace. The journey took several days, allowing for Sam to rest in between stints. Each time they stopped, they dropped anchor and fished. They had managed to find a metal grate within which to cook, with the aid of Nikki and his power of fire. It was a tough journey but with Marta's management and the guidance of the voice they had survived to their destination.

As they approached the island they were aware that they had been spotted. The large crowds gathered on the beach were not what they had been expecting. Having kept themselves hidden so much they were suddenly exposed and vulnerable to whatever might happen. Marta had an ocean between her and the earth, Nikki could not use excessive fire for fear of destroying their vessel, which only left Sam being able to send them in a different direction, away from where they needed to be. They could only hope that the large crowds on the beach would be friendly and that the girl they had come for, was nearby. As they got closer, they could see the islanders becoming more frenzied. Then they witnessed something that they were not expecting as a young and beautiful girl, summoned the sea and created a throne that carried her towards them. She arrived and greeted them and at once they were put at ease as they realised this was who they were here for. Marta decided to be the one to respond to her greeting as the boys had already become transfixed by the beautiful woman, floating before them, and were struggling to muster any words.

"Well I'm certainly glad you are expecting us. We were a bit worried by the large crowd on the beach. There are quite a lot of people that aren't so pleased to see us, you know. Mainly soldiers. So, I am Marta and these two lame looking guys are Sam and Nikki but you probably already know that."

"I do, the voice has kept me informed. I am Namaka."

"Great! I wish he would keep me as informed."

"Our connection is strong and has been since my very early years." Namaka responded.

"Brilliant! So, I see that you are very much in control of your powers and even have a throne. I've got to say that is very cool and I wish I had thought of that."

"Thank you. I shall move you onto the beach where we can talk some more and get to know each other. Forgive my friends on the beach, they haven't seen outsiders in a very long time and they are going to be very curious. But they mean well and are very loving."

With that, Namaka turned towards the beach and floated ahead of them as she steered them in.

"So you two pathetic looking guys can close your gaping mouths now." Marta snapped at Sam and Nikki. "Yes she is beautiful but way out of your league. Anyone would think you hadn't seen a woman before. Hello! I'm right here!"

"Sorry Marta." Sam responded. "It's not that you're not attractive. You are, it's just with you it's like …"

"Being with your mother!" Nikki interjected and then let out a raucous laugh. Sam tried to stifle his laughter so as to not offend Marta but Nikki was correct in his statement as far as he was concerned.

Marta threw them a look that was becoming familiar to them. That of disappointment, which immediately put them in their place and got them concentrating at the task in hand. Inside Marta was revelling in the power that she had over them and was not really upset by the mother comment. She was fond of them both, particularly Sam who had very much become a little brother to her. Nikki was a bit tougher but had proved valuable on the journey and always contributed well to what was needed. Being alone for so long meant that he wasn't as open emotionally but maybe time would change that.

As they approached the beach Namaka had arrived already and was talking to the islanders. She was presumably putting them at ease at the sudden arrival of outsiders and as they landed ashore, they were helped out of the boat and guided towards the waiting crowd who treated them with excitement; as though they were relatives arriving after a long time away. Nikki and Sam were definitely enjoying the attention. After all it had been just the three of them for quite some time and different people to interact with was something to make the most of.

"Come on you two, stop falling behind." Called Marta. "It definitely is like having to keep an eye on two kids Namaka."

"Unfortunately she can be quite bossy at times." Nikki said to Namaka. "I don't know about you but I find it annoying sometimes. It will be nice to have someone like yourself with us for a change."

"I don't know, I think she's marvellous. I am looking forward to spending more time with her. Nothing better than a strong, independent woman." Namaka then moved ahead of the boys to join with Marta. "I am going to have to give a speech to my people and explain in full what is going on. I knew this day was coming but they had no idea. They aren't really aware of the situation going on in the world. We are so isolated here. It's going to take some explaining. That I will have to leave with you."

"Ok I suppose I will let you do your thing and not interfere." Replied Marta.

With that Namaka stood upon a rock and gathered everyone around.

"My friends, today is a day full of emotion. There is a lot of joy in welcoming our guests to the island. They have come a long way from the mainland and we will be able to show them how wonderful our life is here. That is a lot to be grateful for and we can be proud of how we live here. There are also other emotions that we will have to contend with. Our guests, like me, have powers. They control the earth, the wind and fire. With me, we complete a necessary connection with which we can heal our world. A world that is very much in need of our help. Away from this island there are many troubles and people need us. They need us to take away the hurt and suffering that they have endured over many years. Therefore, this day also brings some sadness. Soon I will have to leave you for a while and go with our new friends in order to achieve this goal. You will be well looked after and the elders of this magnificent island will guide you all. You will be safe from the dangers of the outside world but only if I no longer remain here. The evil, that is present, will come looking for me, just as it has sought out these three brave warriors that have joined us today. For now though we must look after our guests and help them recover from the hardships that they have endured. Let's not think of sadness but of joy as this is only a signal of even better times to come. It has always been my pleasure to serve my people and I will continue to do so for the rest of my life. So let's eat and drink like we always do but party as well tonight in honour of our guests!"

Namaka climbed down off the rock and was immediately swarmed upon by the gathered crowd. Understandably, they were confused and concerned about what she had just said. She reassured them and answered their questions, taking time to bring comfort to all. Marta, Nikki and Sam looked on, impressed with the manner with which she dealt with the islanders. She was so young yet seemed to have wisdom way beyond her years.

"I have to admit she is very impressive." Nikki said. "But is she aware that saying, she is only leaving for a while isn't likely to be true? In fact none of us may ever return home again."

"I think she knows. She just doesn't want to worry her people. Be careful what you say whilst we are here, we don't want to scare anyone." Marta replied. The boys agreed and waited patiently whilst Namaka dealt with the islanders.

When she had finished, she managed to break away and return to Marta and the boys.

"Come now, I will show you where you will be staying. I'm sure you are exhausted and need to take a bath and rest."

"Bath!" exclaimed Marta. "I haven't had one of those in such a long time. It sounds like heaven. Do boys even know how to use one of those?" Marta chuckled as they were led into the town where the islanders lived.

As they passed through the town, they noticed how well maintained it was.

"I haven't seen anything like this before. It's amazing!" Sam gushed.

"Yes, I suppose it is to anyone not from here. I can only imagine what the mainland is like, as I have been here all my life. Not a lot has changed here. We used to get supply ships arriving but they stopped coming and we soon learnt of what was going on around the world from a few that escaped and arrived on our shores. So, we adapted our way of life. We no longer had electricity or fossil fuels so we returned to the ways of old. We are completely self-sufficient here and I suppose the things we no longer have weren't good for us anyway. We still have shops but no money. So, people can still acquire things so long as their household has enough in their rations. Everyone is entitled to an equal amount, even me. Everyone has a job suited to their skills, whether it be to fish or farm. Some make clothes, some teach, whatever is needed to maintain a normal society. If we didn't have such a great mission ahead of us, I would say to come and stay with us and spend the rest of your days living this life. Unfortunately, that is not what has been chosen for us. So, I suggest we take a few days to enjoy ourselves and then get ready for what lies ahead."

The group arrived at a large house in the middle of the town. In comparison to what Marta, Nikki and Sam had seen previously in their lifetimes, this was palatial. A solid built house with all its walls intact; a roof, windows and doors.

"This is where you will be staying with me. It once housed my parents as well but they found it difficult having their child being treated the way I am, so decided to move out of the town to a much more secluded area. It is better for all that way. At least when I get to see them I can just be their child again without all the fuss of leading the islanders. So, there is plenty of room for you guys to take it easy for a few days and recover."

She led them into the house, which downstairs was very open and spacious, giving plenty of room for Namaka to hold meetings with the elders of the island. It was well maintained and contained plenty of furniture in good condition. The group were amazed as they walked through. They hadn't seen anything like this before. Occasionally, at least one of them would sit themselves down on a comfortable chair and sink into it, before they were led on to another room on their guided tour. Each room impressed them and it seemed like they had arrived in a form of wonderland but the best was yet to come. Namaka led them upstairs to show them where they would sleep. Each had their own room containing something quite magical, a bed.

Namaka showed the boys their rooms first and the moment they discovered their individual spaces, they immediately leapt onto their beds and started hugging and caressing the pillows and sheets in a sort of ritual that created the image of someone greeting a lost love. Each time, the girls gave confused looks to the boys, then understanding glances to each other and left them to it.

"Finally we have the best room that I have saved for you." Namaka addressed Marta.

Namaka flung open the door to the most luxurious room that Marta had ever seen or could have imagined. In the centre was a large four poster bed with white sheets and pillows. The mattress was thick and deep enough to sink into for a lifetime. The sun shone into the room highlighting the plush furniture and the shiny wooden floors. It was the most amazing room that Marta had ever seen.

"It was my parent's room and my mother's favourite place to be. She would spend hours seated by the window, reading or sewing. Sometimes, she would just sit and watch the world go by from there. It's nice to have someone special in here again."

Marta was hesitant, not because she didn't want to just dive onto the bed just as the boys had done but she was aware that after days at sea she was in a bit of a state. She was extremely dirty and did not smell very nice. She didn't want to make a mess of such a lovely room.

"I appreciate this, I really do. But I can't. Look at the state of me, I would ruin such a beautiful room." Marta pointed out, embarrassed.

"I've already thought of that. The great thing about this room is that it has its own bathroom attached and I made sure that someone came ahead, heated the water and filled all the baths." Namaka then opened an adjoining door to display a deep, porcelain bath filled with hot water. "So get out of those dirty clothes and I will get them washed and repaired. It's time for you to take it easy for a while. You have got everyone to this stage so far but there is so much more to do. We need you to recover for a while."

Without hesitation, Marta stripped off her dishevelled clothes and proceeded to climb into the bath. As she did so she suddenly realised that she had done so in front of a relative stranger and suddenly felt vulnerable and apologetic.

"I'm sorry, I have got so used to getting by with the boys around it didn't occur to me that I shouldn't be just taking my clothes off in front of you like that."

"That's ok, I suppose I will have to get used to it. In fact it is nice that you already feel comfortable with me here."

"I do actually." Replied Marta.

"Good. Well I suppose you and I are destined to become close, so I doubt there will be any boundaries between us. In fact, if I think about it, I'm sure we will be very happy. Now, I had better leave you to rest. Take your time and I will get some food sent up. I should think we will join the islanders tonight for some fun."

Namaka picked up Marta's clothes, smiled at her in a caring fashion and left. Marta then sank further down into the bath, allowing the water to cover her. She was aware that she was so dirty that the water was quickly turning brown in colour but she didn't care. She would make sure she had several baths over the next few days; as many as she could fit in. For the first time in a long time she felt safe and secure. No one was coming to bother her for now and she could just let the stress wash away with the dirt.

Chapter Nineteen

Freedom

Marta awoke refreshed. She had never slept in bed as comfortable as the one she just had. It was like being hugged and supported all over and as such she had slept long and deep. She wasn't sure how long she had been asleep but it was dark now and outside was lit up from small fires burning away. Someone had been in while she was dreaming and had left fresh clothes hanging on the front of the old, grand wardrobe opposite her. Although she couldn't see down to the street level from the bed, she could sense that there was a party atmosphere coming from down below. She wrapped the bedsheet around her and moved towards the window to take a closer look, and there she could see plenty of fun going on.

She quickly changed into the clothes that had been left for her. A long flowing dress in bright colours, not something she was used to wearing and certainly not something that she would go to battle in. Her hair, although now clean, was a mess from her long uninterrupted sleep and she hastily tried to make it look better, eventually adding a scarf around her head to give her an intentional bohemian look. Then she rushed out of the bedroom and down the stairs to join the crowds gathered outside. As she exited the house she paused on the porch, at the entrance, to survey all that was going on. There she could see that Sam and Nikki were already deeply immersed in the party atmosphere; dancing and drinking without a care in the world. Their abandonment of any worries or stresses was a glorious sight to see. They were safe here for the time being and they had discovered something that they had not experienced in a long time, if at all, freedom. As she watched over what was going on she heard and then saw someone who was now becoming familiar, Namaka.

"Well there she is, our very own sleeping beauty, and now she looks like a beautiful princess rather than a street urchin. Wow, you scrub up well."

Marta liked the compliment but was also slightly embarrassed by the flattery. The boys weren't ones for saying such things to her, as her main purpose to them was as a fellow warrior.

"Thank you. I don't think I have ever worn anything this beautiful before, so I am not sure that it is me you should be complimenting but rather the dress." Marta replied.

"Nonsense, it's all you. I checked on you earlier, but you were sound asleep, so I thought it best to leave you. Sorry that we started the party without you."

"That's ok I am grateful of the rest. I don't think I have slept like that since I was a child."

"Well I do have to say you did look rather angelic sleeping there and there I was thinking that you were a bad girl." Namaka laughed as she spoke.

"I have my moments but then I have to be tough with Nikki and Sam around. How are they doing? Have they been behaving themselves?"

"Stop being a mother, Marta. They are doing just fine, maybe a bit too much to drink, especially Sam but they are having fun."

"Sorry, I can't help myself. I suppose now that we have you I don't need to worry so much."

"And you also have someone that can pay attention to you now." Namaka replied. "Come on now, let's get some food and drink into you. It's time for you to join the fun." With that she took Marta by the hand and led her into the middle of the party.

Sam and Nikki had been enjoying themselves. It was a nice change for them to be in centre of everything and not have to hide from danger. They were a bit taken aback when they saw Marta.

"Wow, check you out!" Sam gasped.

"Yeah, the mum scrubs up pretty fine." Nikki joked.

"Err, thank you, I think." Replied Marta. "I trust that you two have been behaving yourselves, while I haven't been around?"

"No guarantees." Replied Nikki. "Now that you're here Namaka, perhaps you can make her a bit easier to be with and a little less bossy. You could show her how to be just as fine as you are." Nikki sidled up to Namaka in an attempt to be a bit flirty in his slightly drunken state.

"Thank you Nikki, I appreciate the compliment. But personally I think Marta is just about perfect as she is."

"Yeah, but you're much more my kind of woman. I mean you are so beautiful." As Nikki said this, Sam sniggered behind him, aware that Nikki had probably made an ill-fated move.

"Well thank you Nikki, you are very handsome yourself but unfortunately you are definitely not my type."

"How so?"

"Well you are a man, which pretty much sums it up."

Nikki took a moment before it sank in. He then stood motionless, wondering what to do with himself.

"Now then you two, there are a lot of young women that are desperate to talk to you. They want to know all about you and the outside world on the mainland. So I suggest you don't disappoint them by wasting your time with me and Marta. After all you're going to be spending a lot of time with us, you need to be generous with your time to those that won't have the opportunity that we two lucky girls will have."

With that Sam turned Nikki around and pulled him into the waiting crowd, in order to continue partying and follow Namaka's instructions.

"I hope you don't mind me ordering those two around. It seems like you could do with a break from it for a while."

"Not at all! Be my guest! It can be very tiring, trying to keep those two out of trouble. I am more than happy with the help. Mind you, I do have to admit that I am quite fond of them." Marta responded.

"I can see that. Now we had better get some food and drink before it all goes. While you were sleeping the voice and I had a chat. Don't worry we weren't cutting you out, we just thought you could do with the rest. We reckon we can be here for a few days before we have to move on. Lyra won't make the effort to send anybody here for the moment, as she is busy building up her forces, which means we are going to have to act soon before she is too strong. So let's get ourselves sorted and ready."

"Ok. It's nice to have someone else making some decisions and I suppose it is best that we have some fun and recuperate. It will make us stronger. To be honest I am so happy to have you with us now. I hope you don't mind me asking but what you said to Nikki about not liking boys, is that true or were you just trying to put him off?"

"That's true, just never felt that way about them."

"Cool. Shall we dance? I just feel the need to dance!" With that Marta dragged Namaka towards where the music was in full flow and the crowds were in full festival spirit.

As they reached the centre of the action Marta flung her arms in the air and screamed in full jubilation. Namaka summoned someone to bring them some drinks and on its arrival Marta swallowed it down in one. Realising that she was going to be in full party mode Namaka gave instructions to keep the food and drink flowing for their guest. Marta was determined to enjoy herself as much as she could, as she wouldn't know when she might get the chance again. She gyrated to the beat of the music, allowing it to take control of her and as she became more intoxicated by the music and the drink she clung on to Namaka for support. This was Marta's new friend and she was happy to keep her close. For now she had not a care in the world, she was enjoying the freedom she had in this moment. Tomorrow could wait.

Chapter Twenty

Together

After a few days, the four had bonded well. They enjoyed each other's company and were happy that they were going to be able to work together. Each day, they had enjoyed all that the island had to offer, the weather, the tranquillity, the food but most of all the company. They were becoming a well-balanced group, comfortable that they would protect and care for each other no matter what happened. Life was good but they all knew it would have to come to an end. As much as they could quite happily have lived the rest of their days on the island, this was not the life chosen for them. They must travel again and face whatever came. This was their life, this was their sacrifice. To stay would put the island at risk, as Lyra would not just let them live there without attacking at some point. They were too strong and too much of a risk. Namaka knew this day would come and was well prepared. She had put some islanders to work on preparing all that they would need. She took the rest of the gang down to the beach to ready them for their departure.

When they arrived at the seafront a magnificent sight was there to greet them. No longer would they be travelling in the broken down yacht that they had arrived in, because in front of them was the most wonderful vessel they had seen. Much larger than their last boat, this was definitely built for ocean sailing. Tall sails flying high above the large boat beneath. Enough space for them to live comfortably and to hold supplies for a year. This was luxury compared to what they were used to but just as much as they would have expected from Namaka and the islanders. It was clear why they had come here last, because this was the place that got them prepared for the really tough times to come.

"This used to be a supply ship back in the day but it has been long time since we used it for that. I made sure we kept it maintained for a time such as this. I hope you like it." Namaka explained.

"It's wonderful. Thank you." Marta responded. "In fact everything here has been wonderful, it is such a shame we have to leave. I hope everyone understands how grateful we are."

The boys nodded in agreement as they looked upon the islanders gathered around.

"They understand, and they are all sad to see us leave. Take the rowboat out to the ship and I will join you there after I have said my final goodbyes."

The three of them climbed into the rowboat and headed to the ship. As they did so, they watched Namaka say her tearful goodbyes. Her parents had returned to the town, at her request, and would be involved in the running of the island whilst she was gone. She hugged all that wished to do so, leaving her parents till last. As the others approached the ship they witnessed the difficulty Namaka was having in leaving her loved ones behind. They had all been in that situation, so they could understand the turmoil and pain that she was going through.

They boarded the ship and began to look around at all the wonders that the vessel provided. Occasionally they each glanced back at the shore to see how Namaka was doing. It was a private moment so they didn't wish to intrude but all of them were fond of her, so they wanted to keep an eye none the less.

When her goodbyes were done and she had managed to escape the final clutches of her parents, Namaka walked into the sea. The moment she touched the water it swept her up into the throne that she so often used and bore her across to the boat, eventually placing her down on the deck.

She stood motionless for a while, as did the others, taking time to realise the gravity of the moment.

"You alright?" Marta asked. Namaka said nothing, instead she forced a smile at Marta that said it all. "That's ok, we understand." Marta then hugged and held her, allowing for the moment to happen with the knowledge that they all cared. The boys then surrounded the girls and encased them in a huge group hug. They all paused for a moment to experience one last moment of calm before Marta took control once more.

"Right let's get going so I don't get stuck under Sam's armpit anymore." This immediately brought a smile to everyone's face and broke up the huddle. "Only kidding Sam, you smell quite nice. It must have been all those baths in order to impress the girls, if only your mum could see you now." Sam smiled, somewhat embarrassed at being so easily caught out by what Marta had said.

"So who is going first? Is Sam going to bring up the wind or are you going to use the water?" Marta asked.

"Neither." Namaka replied. "We will need to conserve all the energy we can, so we will sail naturally."

"Ok. Well we are on water, so I guess you're the boss."

"Not at all my dear. Just my suggestion. Anyway who is in a rush to get to the mainland? I am very happy not to and then I get some more quality time with you all." The boys agreed with this too. Marta smiled as she realised that Namaka was always going to be able to charm her way around her too.

"What actually is next for us?" Sam asked. "I know we are heading to the mainland and it is going to be dangerous but what are we going to do? Surely the four of us can't just take on all the troops on our own. Do we need to build an army ourselves or are there more like us with powers that we need to get?"

"There is another that you must collect but the journey there is the toughest yet." Interjected the voice.

"Awesome who is next?" Nikki interrupted.

"It is time that we all came together." Said the voice.

"It's you. We are coming to get you aren't we?" Marta responded, realising what the voice was saying.

"You are. In order for us to heal all that is wrong in the world we must be complete and we must have balance. However, getting to me will not be easy. Lyra has grown stronger by the day and her armies are growing in number. She will do anything to stop us from being together because once that happens we will be stronger and much more of a force against her."

"Don't worry we will get to you." Marta replied as the others agreed.

"We had better get a move on then." Said Namaka. "I suggest we divide into teams. You boys can take the first stint whilst Marta and I rest down below."

"Don't you think we should have one boy and one girl, in case something happens? You might need one of us guys, just in case." Nikki responded.

The look from Marta and Namaka was swift and sharp. Both of them were appalled by his suggestion that they may need a man with them. Namaka took swift action, and with a flick of her wrist a wave flew over the side of the boat and drenched Nikki in sea water.

"Hey I thought we said that no powers were to be used." Nikki protested in his now wet state, whilst Sam shrieked with laughter.

"You're right Nikki, but it was a moment where I couldn't control my emotions. You see that's what happens when I am confronted with stupidity like that." Namaka replied.

"Alright, alright, I'm sorry. You two go and chill whilst Sam and I sort things out." With that the girls went below deck laughing with each other.

Days passed at sea on their long journey; each taking their turns in sailing towards their destination. They managed to rest and eat well on their journey, as there were ample supplies provided by the islanders. It was a special time for all of them. They got to know each other some more and they grew tighter as a group with each passing moment. They learned what each one of them had come from and what it would mean if they lost the battles ahead and as such, it strengthened their resolve to give everything for each other. The voice guided them on the route that they needed to take, regularly warning them of the dangers ahead.

After many days, they sighted land in the distance and started their journey in. However, as they approached land the sight was not what they hoped for. As far as they could see a massive army was stretched along the coastline. They had been expecting danger and that they would encounter it the moment they reached land but nothing on this scale. The beach was full of soldiers armed and ready. Above them on the clifftop were even more, their number must have been in the thousands. Worst of all, in the centre, was the most fearful sight that they could have expected, ready and waiting for their arrival; Lyra.

Chapter Twenty-One

The Battle

Lyra looked down upon her amassed armies and out into the ocean, where she could see the ship that they had been waiting for. She had been busy in recent times. Aware that she was about to come up against a force, like none she had encountered before, she had been recruiting and bolstering her forces. Town by town, city by city she had been displaying the full force of her armies and of her powers. Little choice was given to anybody they had come across. They must join her in her quest or face the consequences. If they did not easily understand that they had to join her, then Lyra's powers of mind control were used instead. Regardless, joining up and fighting was the only thing that could be done. As such Lyra had created the largest and most powerful army imaginable. It stretched out for miles along the coastline; fearsome and ready to vanquish their oncoming enemy, armed and ready to fight for her and their own future survival.

On the ship the four looked at what they were expected to face. None had expected this. They knew that the next stage of their journey would be dangerous. They knew that in order to achieve their goal they would encounter the armies of Lyra but nothing had prepared them for the scale and magnitude of this. As they looked at what they were about to face, the fear took hold of them and they started then to look at each other for answers.

"Surely we don't have to fight that. Is there not a way round them?" Sam shouted to the others.

"There is no way of avoiding them" replied the voice. "You could sail along the coast and the armies would just follow, waiting for you to land. Eventually, you would run out of supplies and they could just starve you. You have to get past them and travel on, through the mainland, to reach me."

"Right, so blasting the hell out of them is the only way to go." Responded Nikki.

"I would recommend some caution in your tactics. You have to remember that many of those that fight for Lyra are not there because of free will. Many have families like you, and are only here because they have to be."

"Are you kidding me?" Nikki fired back. "You want us to defeat that massive army and get past them but try not to hurt them!"

"Some will be hurt" replied the voice, "but those that deserve it are the ones closest to Lyra and they will not be putting themselves at risk. They will be giving the instructions."

"So basically we need to get to those up on the clifftop." Marta interjected. "This certainly isn't going to be easy. Sounds like we need to divide and conquer."

"Exactly Marta." Replied the voice.

"Well I hate to say this but it doesn't look like we have much time to come up with a plan. Take a look." Shouted Nikki, who was pointing out what was happening on the beach. There they could see hundreds of archers loading up with arrows. As the boat sailed closer to the shore they waited for the order to fire. Then that order came. Hundreds of arrows flew up into the air like a tidal wave heading towards them.

"Ok boys you're up!" Marta cried. "Sam blow them away from us and Nikki anything he doesn't get turn it to ashes.

"I thought you'd never ask." Nikki shouted excitedly.

As Sam began to divert as many of the arrows away from them Nikki fired up his flames and began to throw up fireballs to destroy any that were left. Wave by wave the arrows came flying towards them each time being defeated by the boys and their skills.

Lyra watched from on top of the clifftop at what was happening. She smiled and spoke to her commanders.

"How pathetic! They have the power to hurt us but they are too afraid and too weak. You see that there is no real leadership amongst them. No ruthless streak. That is why they will always be the losers and I shall rule. Now it is time to step up the fun and games. Let's see what they will do next when they can no longer keep playing defence?"

Lyra had seen what Sam and Nikki were doing and decided to take control. She concentrated her powers on them and began to sing to herself whilst she did so. On the ship the boys had been doing well whilst Marta and Namaka tried to figure out a way out of this situation.

Suddenly the boys began to fade, then they fell to the floor screaming in agony and holding their heads.

"What's happened?" screamed Marta.

"Lyra has got into their heads and is torturing them." Replied the voice.

"Can't you do something about it?"

"I can. I will block her but it will take all that I have to combat it. You will be on your own."

"That's fine just do it. Just save them will you!" Marta barked at the voice. Without the boys' defences, the arrows were now raining down on the ship, tearing through the sails and wedging into the deck. Marta and Namaka dragged the boys under cover saving themselves as well at the same time.

"Right we can't just sit here and wait to be defeated, time to do something." Marta cried out. "Namaka I need you to wash some waves up onto the shore. Try and take out the archers for the moment. At least that should stop them for the moment while we think of something else."

"Can do" replied Namaka. Who immediately rushed to the side of the boat and summoned huge waves sending them crashing down upon the coastline. Each wave battered the troops, knocking them off their feet as they tried to reload. Each time they recovered themselves another wave would hit them, rendering them useless.

Lyra could witness what was happening, whilst she also battled with the voice who was blocking her signals. She realised it was time for the next wave of attack and she gestured to her commanders to load up with the more effective artillery that was amassed on the clifftop.

Back on the boat Marta and Namaka could see the activity that was happening.

"I don't think me drenching the beaches is going to be much use soon. Any ideas?" Namaka called out to Marta who was trying to comfort the boys through their anguish.

"Well I wish I was an expert on how to divide and conquer." She replied. Then it came to her. "I have got it! We need to split them up. We have to get Lyra and the commanders away from the rest of the troops and then get through them"

"Ok and how are we going to do that?"

"We leave them stranded on an island!" Marta excitedly shouted as a plan had finally come together in her mind. Namaka looked confused as she stared at Marta. Then the plan started to work its way into her mind.

"Do you think you can do that?" Namaka asked.

"Well we are about to find out."

Marta left the boys and came to the side of the boat. What she was about to do was going to take more power than she had used before and she was afraid of what might happen.

"When I give you the signal I am going to need you to redirect the waves and help me out." Marta instructed Namaka.

Then when she was ready Marta summoned her powers and began to get to work. She then began to concentrate on the earth surrounding Lyra and her commanders. As she did so the ground began to crack and split apart all around them, shaking and throwing them from their feet. Lyra screamed as she realised what was happening but was powerless to act as the voice was combatting her powers, leaving her helpless.

Bit by bit the clifftop began to tear away from the mainland, leaving them alone on a small piece of land. More and more the void became bigger as they started to separate from where the rest of the troops were gathered and they were beginning to become isolated.

Back on the boat Marta was concentrating with all she had at her disposal but each moment was taking its toll on her.

"Ok I need you now, Namaka"

On her instruction, Namaka moved the waves away from the now sodden troops on the beach. They were very much broken and unable to continue the fight. She then moved the waves and directed them into the cracks that Marta has created on the mainland. Quickly and powerfully the waves moved, eroding further the area surrounding Lyra and the commanders. Panic was taking hold on the small piece of land and some threw themselves off hoping for a way out, only to be swept up by the now raging torrent surrounding them. Whilst all others around her were in a state of commotion Lyra composed herself and stared out to sea at those who battled against her. Strangely, she appeared almost proud of those she looked upon. She knew for now that she was beaten but seemed to be aware that this would not be the last time, she would fight against them. They were worthy opponents.

Piece by piece the land tore away from the mainland and was no longer grounded by the earth. The small strip, that Lyra and her commanders were on, was now an island floating on the sea. Marta and Namaka had successfully stranded them and now all that was left to do was send them further away. Namaka summoned the seas and lifted them further and further out into the ocean. The distress could be seen and heard from all except one, Lyra. As they were swept away she remained motionless, continuing to stare at those who had defeated her until she could be seen no more.

Although the girls had succeeded, there was no time to celebrate as they still had to get past the troops on the sea. Some would still be loyal to Lyra and would try to carry on their attack. Therefore, landing on the shore would not be safe and they still needed to pass.

Once more Marta summoned her powers and began to bore into the mainland. This time her efforts were to create a river to sail down and pass the troops. As she split the land apart once more she was aided by Namaka sending the waters crashing into any gaps created. The power of their combined forces soon opened up a large gap between the troops, leaving them stranded either side of the developing river. Wider and wider it grew, then longer and longer as the earth and water created the river inland. Further and further they developed the river and when the moment came Namaka began to use the waves to push them along the river, at speed, and past the troops. Mile after mile they carried on, fearing that if they stopped too soon, some of the troops would catch up to them and seek revenge. Hour after hour they continued their task until there was nothing left to give and eventually Marta swayed and collapsed backwards, falling into the arms of Namaka who subsequently fell to the floor with her cradled in her arms.

"I think we are done now." Said Namaka. "We should be far enough away. Time for you to rest my dear." Marta looked up at her and smiled. She had nothing left to give and no words to say. As she looked up at Namaka she drifted off, overcome with exhaustion.

Namaka looked around at the damaged and battered ship. Its broken appearance was very much representative of the passengers that it carried. She laid down Marta and gathered up some blankets and pillows. She covered and propped up all of her companions to make them as comfortable as possible and then sat watching over them. She was aware that someone needed to stand guard and keep them safe. Although she was exhausted herself, the relatively easier life she had on the island had maybe given her a little more energy. There was no response from the voice either, presumably exhausted from the battle with Lyra. Alone with no idea where they were or what was next to come Namaka had no options other than to sit and wait.

No date, no time, no location.

Chapter Twenty-Two

The Healing

Namaka sat for a long time as night descended, fearful that they would be found but as the time passed no one came. Perhaps the remaining troops had fled. Maybe realising that Lyra had floated away with her commanders and they no longer needed to worry about what might happen to them. Maybe they were too afraid to seek out Namaka and the rest, worried that without Lyra they could not combat others with powers. Whatever the reason, time passed and no one came. If they had, they would have found a team broken and in need of repair.

Namaka sat frightened and alone, wondering what to do. She waited quietly and patiently for the others to recover but as the hours passed there seemed to be no sign of this happening. Was she the only one left? Had the battle damaged the others too much? Was this the end and they had failed? Night followed the day and the stars shone down brightly on the ruined boat and crew, whilst Namaka pondered what she should do. Maybe she could get the ship back to her island and seek help for the others. Or maybe all was already lost and she should just allow the waves to take her home alone. Many thoughts meandered through her mind, as there was nothing else to do in the depths of night.

As time passed, night became day once more and she watched as the sun rose upon them. She looked across at her stricken friends but there was no sign of recovery. They lay motionless where they had fallen, still breathing, still alive but in a form of coma. How long could she remain idle, helpless to do anything about their current state? She needed inspiration. She needed contact of some form.

She moved to the edge of the deck and looked down at the waters, the only other connection she knew. She climbed over the rail and dived in. As she hit the water and sunk down into the depths she felt the connection that she craved. The water bathed her and caressed her, caring for her needs. As she connected with it she began to discover the answers she needed. The water healed her, gave her energy and this was what the others needed, connection to the elements that gave them their powers.

As soon as she had revitalised herself Namaka returned to the ship realising what she had to do. Firstly she moved Sam to a higher position on deck. Previously she had kept him covered and protected, but he needed to be exposed to the wind, allowing it to blow around him and heal him just like the water had done to her. Next she lit a fire in the grate and placed Nikki next to it, certain that this would do what was required. Lastly and most importantly to Namaka, with the aid of the water she swept up Marta and moved her to the land. There she covered her body in the surrounding earth, all the time hoping that her plan would work. She did not know how long it would take but she was sure it would work, just like the water had returned the energy to her. No matter how long, it would be worth the wait if her friends recovered, especially her dear Marta.

So once again Namaka waited hour upon hour, guarding her friends faithfully. Checking on their progress and hoping that her plan would come to fruition. Whilst waiting she remembered the fun times they had already enjoyed, in the short time that they had known each other and day dreamed about what might happen in the future. Would they all find happiness one day? Maybe they would survive all this and live the rest of their days until they were old, enjoying each other's company.

Slowly, colour seemed to return to the complexion of Sam and Nikki. Maybe they were not so hurt by the battle but there definitely seemed to be signs of something happening. Not a lot seemed to change with Marta. She and Namaka had become so close and had formed such a strong bond that she couldn't imagine being without her. As such, Namaka stayed by Marta as much as she could, whilst regularly checking on the boys. Eventually, there was a glimmer of hope, not from Marta but from Sam. He began to stir and occasionally awoke, only to mumble a bit and return to a deep sleep. The same began to happen with Nikki and all the time Namaka attended to them at the slightest sign of recovery. Still she waited. Yet again night fell and yet again she sat and wished for better times. Eventually, she could no longer stay awake and she drifted off into a deep sleep by the side of Marta.

Morning broke once more and as the sunlight hit Namaka she awoke suddenly and was startled, as she hadn't meant to fall asleep. She hastily checked on Marta who was still laying by her side. Afraid that she had left her duties, she hurriedly returned to the ship to check on the boys. She stoked the fire by Nikki and checked on him. He looked healthier, which comforted her a little and then she went to check on Sam. As she approached, she was startled to see that his eyes were open and staring across the deck.

"Sam!" she shrieked upon realising he was awake. "Are you ok?" In her excitement she grasped hold of him and began to hold him tight against her.

"I would be if you weren't smothering me." Sam replied. Namaka slowly laid him down apologetically, realising that her excitement was too much. "Well if I am in the afterlife that was a good start. Although no offence to you, I would of preferred Marta." Sam laughed at his own joke whilst Namaka twisted her face in disapproval.

"Well I see your sense of humour hasn't improved so you must be getting back to normal." Namaka retorted.

"I'm ok I think. My head seems ok but my body just seems to be telling me to lay here and rest. It is not ready to move yet. How is everyone else?"

Just as he said that Nikki came staggering onto the deck, his legs barely able to carry him until he found a spot to collapse once more. Namaka ran to him and helped him to a comfortable position.

"Well that answers any questions about Nikki." Sam responded. "Hey fella, I see you didn't get any better looking during your recovery."

"Same with you I see." Nikki fired back.

"Right, so I see you two are the same idiots as before." Namaka retorted back, in the manner she had seen from Marta so often. "So you two need to carry on resting and I will get you some food. Don't move either of you!"

"Wow you sound like Marta." Responded Sam. "Where is she?"

"Still recovering. So I need you two to behave while I look after her." Namaka didn't want to say too much, as the boys still needed to rest and not to worry.

Namaka fed the boys and return to Marta hoping that there might be some change but unlike the boys there didn't seem to be much of a difference. How long would it take she wondered? So, she did her best to split her time between Marta and the boys, continuing to care for them all.

Later, as she sat once more by Marta's side, she could feel a gust of wind followed by the sound of footsteps and a couple of shadows creeping over her as they blocked out the sun.

"You two need to work on being stealthier when trying to sneak up on people." Namaka called out, aware that Sam and Nikki were behind her.

"And you need to work on your skills of lying to us about Marta" Nikki responded.

"I didn't want you to worry. You need rest."

"Let us decide that. You need rest too." Said Nikki. As he did so he gathered up some wood and started a fire. Namaka smiled as she realised that the team was coming back together. Sam handed her a pillow and some blankets, aware that if they were to get Namaka to rest, it would only be by Marta's side. She accepted that they were now taking charge and without argument she cuddled up to Marta and drifted off to sleep, while the boys kept watch. Night fell once more and the boys kept watch over the girls.

As dawn broke once more, there was a quiet breeze in the air and the smoke from the burnt-out fire mixed with it to gently swirl around. This was what Marta first saw when she opened her eyes. She lay for a while and watched it dance above her. She had no desire to move. Her body had been energised from the earth below her but the warmth came from Namaka pressed against her and it felt good.

As she pushed herself in closer to Namaka she thought she had better make her presence known.

"Morning lovely, have you been waiting long?" Marta whispered to Namaka. In an instant Namaka's eyes opened up wide to check that she wasn't dreaming. She gasped for air as she searched for the words to say but her excitement wouldn't allow anything to come out.

"Don't say anything." Marta whispered. "I am far too comfortable and I don't need those boys to disturb me right now." Namaka did as she was told and quietly cuddled up closer to Marta. She was happy and didn't want to ruin this moment. Finally, they were all healing and life could carry on. They just needed to hear from the voice.

Chapter Twenty-Three

Onward

Days passed whilst the group recovered. They had no idea where they were or what was to happen next. They enjoyed spending time with each other and having no battles to fight was certainly a relief, but time was passing and nothing much was happening. None had heard from the voice in a long time and they began to worry that they were now alone with no direction. Maybe it was over, maybe all they had left to do was to return home but something told all of them there was still a lot to do. The world still needed healing, yet they had no idea how to do it.

Then, after several days, came what they had been waiting for; the voice.

"Hello everyone, I am sorry that I have not been in touch but like you I needed to recover."

"At last! We were beginning to worry." Replied Marta

"I am touched by your concern. However, I am still weak and will remain so, until you reach me. I will need your help as battling with Lyra took much of what I had left. I shall show you the way Marta and then I will leave you until you arrive. I will not be able to sustain communication for much longer."

In an instant, images started flooding Marta's mind. Flashes of pictures battered her, making her stumble as the power of what was happening hit her hard. The rest comforted and supported her, as they could see that the download of information was affecting her deeply and causing her some distress. Marta let out a scream, in the hope of easing the pain it was causing. She knew however, that this was necessary to carry on. Finally, she fell to her knees as she received all the information.

"Don't worry we will get to you." Marta said, realising that she was talking to herself as the voice was no longer there. "I know where we have to go now so we had better get ready. It's going to be a long journey on foot. So, we will need to pack what we can carry and Namaka you are going to have to put a lot more clothes on." Marta smiled at her friend as she said this. Namaka was used to living on an island where the sun shone down all year round, so wearing many clothes was not what she was used to. The boys smiled at this too, as they had been appreciative of Namaka's choice of clothing or lack of it but did wonder if she ever wore much else.

"Shame," said Nikki "it's not right to have to cover up such beauty but we all have to make sacrifices." There was a hint of cynicism in his statement having been quickly rejected by her on the island, yet he still had to view her obvious beauty on a daily basis and that it was never covered.

"That's not a problem, how bad can it be?" Namaka responded.

"Exactly." Replied Marta as she raised her eyebrows. She had seen in her vision the conditions they were about to face and had concerns that her dear friend was not going to do well.

As instructed, they set about getting ready. They packed up as many supplies as they could carry, into backpacks and dressed for heavy weather conditions ahead. Namaka came up from below deck, dressed in whatever she could find. As she didn't usually wear clothes of this sort she had borrowed some from the rest of the group. They were oversized and ill-fitting and she did look a bit ridiculous, like a child that had just raided their parents' wardrobe.

"Look at me, I look so stupid." Namaka exclaimed. The others tried to stifle their laughter, as they did agree but didn't want to make it worse.

"Don't be silly, you look rather cute and cuddly." Marta said. Once more trying not to laugh.

"I think that is about the worst thing you could have said." Namaka responded.

Once they were ready, they began their journey. Only Marta knew where they were going but even she, did not know how long it was going to take. All she knew was they were to head north and keep going. The image that was given to her of their final destination, was a cold and barren place. Not much could survive where they were going and she could only hope that their powers would help them.

Day by day they walked on, stopping only to eat and sleep. The further north they travelled the harsher the conditions they faced. Lush green lands were replaced by frozen and rocky grounds. Occasionally they would have to stop just to allow Nikki to warm them up with his fire, as they huddled together to protect themselves from the conditions. The further they travelled, the harder it became to find food. Day by day they had less to survive on and they grew weak. All of them looked to Marta for some guidance but she had none. She knew that they were heading in the right direction but not how much further. She would only know when they got there.

"How much further? I don't think I can do this much longer." Namaka cried out. "Could the voice not have chosen to live somewhere nicer?"

"I have a feeling it's for a reason." Marta replied.

"Well it had better be a good one."

So, they carried on. As they became weaker the they had to rest for longer periods, cherishing every mouthful of the rations they had left. Each time they covered up and cuddled together they wished that they would never have to split apart again and face the biting cold. They had no idea where they were.

No date, no time, no location.

Marta was becoming concerned. She was beginning to doubt herself. Maybe she was leading them in the wrong direction, maybe she hadn't understood the information correctly. Surely, they must have some answers soon but without the voice there were none. They were not going to be able to carry on for much longer. It was only a matter of days before they would perish in this frozen wasteland. Each step was becoming harder as the conditions underfoot added to the heavy exhaustion of each movement. Perhaps they should turn back before it was too late? Maybe they could try again once they had recovered? All this ran through Marta's mind, fearful that she may fail them all.

All of them were frozen to the bone and could barely walk any more. Sam stumbled and fell to the ground and they rushed to help him. As they huddled together once more, they looked at each other aware of how hopeless their situation was. None of them dared to say what they were all thinking; that they were helplessly stranded and were running out of options or the will to survive.

Once more they covered themselves to protect them from the blizzard conditions that were surrounding them. Sam was now too weak to send the winds away from them and what was once his friend and his supply of power seemed to be turning against them. All they could do was wait and rest once more.

Eventually the blizzard passed over and the sun began to shine on them. Even under the covers, the warmth from the sun could be felt and gave them some relief. They took time to enjoy it before they ventured out once more. After a little while, they realised that they could put it off no more and slowly pulled themselves apart and out from under their cover. As they stood, in the middle of the wasteland, they realised that the conditions were the nicest they had been for a long time and at last all around them was clear and lit up. Suddenly, there was a yell from Marta.

"It's there! I can see it."

Sure enough, in the distance, there was a building of some sort. It looked like it was made of stone but they could not be sure, as it was quite a way from them. Suddenly, there was an energy in the team that had not been there in a long time. No longer did their legs seem so weary and hesitant to walk but instead they were ready to move at a pace, in order to reach their final destination. Quickly, they gathered up everything and headed to the building in the distance. The faster they moved, the larger the building became. What they would discover inside, no one knew. But at this moment in time they didn't care. The end of the journey was in sight and that was all that mattered.

As they got close up to the building it was definitely made of stone. Maybe it had once been more ornate on the outside in days past but the group neither knew, nor cared. It certainly did not look hospitable or in fact like anyone lived there at all. In fact on closer inspection it looked like one thing only. A very grand tomb that someone would be buried inside.

Chapter Twenty-Four

The Voice

The four stood in front of the ornate building before them, yet they had no idea how to proceed.

"It has no doors and windows." Said Nikki. "Have we come all this way to pay our respects to someone or has this been built for us to end our days?"

"I don't know Nikki." Replied Marta, frustrated by the situation that they were in. "It wasn't clear in the images I received. But it does look like you're right. We need to find a way in, even if it is a tomb there must have been a way in. I don't know why the voice has brought us here but it must be for a reason."

The group look around the building until they found what was once a doorway, now blocked by a large rock.

"This is going to take some moving" said Nikki. "Do you want me to blast it?"

"Or we could be a bit more subtle and try to move it more gently. Who knows what is behind it. Let's try to do as little damage as possible." Replied Marta.

With that, she summoned her powers and began to move the earth beneath it, slowly rocking it away from the entrance whilst the other three helped push it aside. Once it had been moved, a vast opening was there before them, leading to a long and dark corridor.

"I think now is the time we need you Nikki. Can you give us some light? I personally don't fancy walking into a tomb in the dark."

Nikki obliged, as he sharpened his swords together and created a couple of torches to light the way. They then proceeded along the dark corridor. Passages sprung out from the sides but they decided to keep going straight on deeper and deeper into the depths of the building. Eventually they reached a set of large doors. They were as ornate as the building outside but this time they were gilded and shined from the light of Nikki's torches.

"This is getting really creepy now. I suppose it's too late to say we should give it a miss and turn back." Sam interjected. He was voicing what by now, all of them were feeling.

"I am afraid not." Marta replied. "Although I can understand why you said that."

"Me too." Namaka added. "I thought we were here to find the voice but it doesn't seem that there is a whole lot of life here right now. I wish were back on the beach at home."

Marta pushed at the door but it wasn't going to move easily. It had obviously been a long time since it was last moved.

"There is a lot blocking the door. If I move the earth from underneath it can you blow it open, Sam?" Marta asked

"I see we are giving up on subtle now." Stated Nikki, sarcastically.

"I think the sooner we get this over with the better." Responded Marta as she used her powers to move the earth, stopping the door from opening. At the same time Sam summoned a gust of wind that came shooting down the corridor from the outside and blasted the doors open and off their hinges.

"Easy fella, not so rough." Nikki joked as Sam looked sheepish at his over enthusiastic blast.

Nikki led the way through the now broken doors and into what appeared to be a vast chamber.

"There seems to be lanterns around the side. Give me a moment whilst I light them up." Nikki then sent out bursts of flame and lit everything up for them all to see.

They realised that they were now standing on the edge of a vast, domed chamber. In the middle of the chamber was an island surrounded by water, and on this island was what could only be described as a coffin seated upon a plinth.

"Well this isn't creepy at all." Stated Sam sarcastically.

"Can you get us across there Namaka?" Marta asked

"I can but are you sure we want to be over there? I am starting to wonder if this is right. I thought we were here to find the voice."

"I have a feeling we may have found what we are looking for." Marta replied.

The group started looking at each other, fearful of what Marta just said. Namaka then controlled the water and swept up Marta, Nikki and herself. Sam gestured that he was fine and took flight over the expanse of water. As they arrived on the central island Nikki was laughing, having enjoyed being lifted up by the water and transported over.

"You missed out there Sam. That was fun." Nikki enthused.

"I decided against having a wet backside mate."

Namaka was not amused by Sam's assessment of her powers and with a flick of the wrist doused him with water from behind. Sam yelled out in shock and disgust.

"I insist you have the team experience." Namaka joked as the others enjoyed a fun moment within the experience they were having. But then they turned more serious and they were drawn to Marta who was surveying what was in front of them.

"I think this is the voice." Marta stated as she looked at the coffin.

"You are correct." Responded the voice. However, this time it could be heard echoing around the domed chamber instead of in their heads.

"So how is that possible? If you are in this coffin how have you been talking to us all this time? Dead people don't just talk to others all over the world."

"I could ask the same of you. How do people such as yourselves control such powers? Not everything is easily explained within what we can understand." Replied the voice. "Just as you control the earth wind, fire and water, my power is to control what cannot be seen, the space between and in your mind. Between you and I, we create the balance in the world and help it to thrive. To live and support all that is here."

"Well it hasn't been going so well lately." Marta responded.

"In each generation there are people such as yourselves and it is their role to create the balance in the world. They will be overseen and guided by one like myself. Eventually, when our natural life is over our powers are passed on. I am from the previous generation and as such, my body no longer exists."

"So why does your voice still exist?" Marta asked.

"When my time was coming to an end, another was born with the same powers that I possess. She was to have taken over from me and guide the next generation, in order to create the balance that was needed. To begin with she listened well and the hope for a better, new world was great. But she faced trauma at a young age and she would no longer be guided by me. She sought to seek revenge on a world that had caused her so much pain."

"Lyra!"

"Indeed Marta. Therefore it was decided that whilst my human form withered and died, my spirit and powers were kept alive by the very chamber that you stand in. This, at least, created a chance that the world could be redeemed and saved from her clutches."

"Something tells me that there is an awful lot still to do." Responded Nikki.

"Yes." Replied the voice. "In order to be of use in our future endeavours I need to be human once more. You must combine your powers to recreate my form. That way we can defeat her and make a better world."

"Ok, tell us what needs to happen. We can do this, right guys?" Marta responded. As she looked around at the others they were not looking that enthusiastic. To them it sounded somewhat dangerous and a leap into the unknown.

"Come on! We can do this! I haven't given so much and come so far to get scared now." Marta pleaded with the others.

"You are asking us to create another with powers like Lyra. She is bad enough. Do we really need another?" Namaka responded. Marta took Namaka by the hand. They had become very close in recent times and she realised that if she could convince her, then the boys would likely follow.

"One day I hope to spend time with you and not have to worry about what awful things might happen in our future." Marta replied whilst looking lovingly at Namaka. "I can't guarantee that what the voice is saying is right. But as far as I can see, this is the only chance we have."

All of them looked at each other and were aware that this may be the only thing to do. Marta's instincts had not let them down before and if it hadn't been for her they wouldn't have come so far. Trust was probably the strongest bond amongst them and now was the time to put it to the test. Marta looked at all of them and from their expressions they were willing to give it a go no matter what the outcome.

"So we have listened to you for so long, it is time to instruct us once more. This time you had better not let us down or I will bury you myself." Marta called out to the voice.

"You must all place your hands upon the box and summon your powers. Concentrate them directly into it where they will combine. The power of the elements that you control will create life within me once more and give me a form, within which I can survive."

"Forgive me now for what damage it may do. Nobody usually survives when I let rip." Nikki exclaimed.

"Hopefully we will be ok." Marta said trying to be reassuring. As they gathered round the coffin, they hugged and touched each other in a consoling fashion, aware that this could be their last chance to show their affection for each other. Then they spread around the coffin, as instructed, and readied themselves for what was about to happen.

"Ok. Let's do this!" Exclaimed Marta as she got ready to put the plan into action.

Nikki lit a spark and placed his hands on the coffin, as did the others. They gave a fleeting last look to each other and then began to concentrate on summoning their powers.

As they all focused they could feel a surge of energy. They realised that in order for them to succeed and remain safe they had to concentrate solely on themselves, regardless of how they felt about each other. The elements began to surge through them and into the coffin. As they continued they began to feel the other elements battering against their own but no matter what, they must not stop. They needed their powers to combine, in order to give life to the voice. As they continued, controlling their powers became more exhausting, still fighting against each other. Then something happened, no longer were the powers fighting against each but beginning to knit together. A vortex was beginning to swirl around them. A spinning combination of the wind, fire, water and earth. The immense pressure was building around them and they began to scream from the agony of what was happening. Yet, they all continued with their task, regardless of the fear and pain that was beginning to take hold of them. They were all aware that they had to succeed or forever live in this wretched world. They had do this for themselves, for their families, for their loved ones.

The vortex surrounding them became stronger and more intense; engulfing them until they could no longer see each other, despite being only centimetres apart. The more intense it became the more the sounds of anguish increased. They yelled for each other to make sure that they were still there and to give themselves the encouragement that they needed to carry on. Faster and faster the vortex of their powers swirled around and through them. More powerful and intense with each passing moment. Deeper and deeper each of them had to dig in order to survive. Until, eventually, a scream, an explosion and then black out.

Chapter Twenty-Five

Life

Marta lay on the floor where she had fallen. She could barely move from the exhaustion and pain that her body was feeling. She had no idea how long she had been laying there as she opened her eyes to look up at the dome she was in. It was different from before. It had been a cold lifeless tomb encasing the voice but now she could see greenery from trees and branches breaking through the walls. Was this even the same place as before? How long had she been lying where she fell? She had no answers.

No date, no time, no location.

As she lay there she began to hear groans. The others were also beginning to awaken. She turned her head to see them and was happy to see that all of them had survived. Slowly and gently they began to get up from the floor and as they did, so they became aware of another figure standing there watching over them.

This figure stood smiling in a welcoming fashion. The figure was dressed only in a sheet and nothing else. They had no hair or any distinguishing features to show who they were. Yet when the figure began to speak they knew who it was.

"I am glad to see you all at last." As the figure spoke they all knew immediately that it was the person they knew as the Voice.

"It's you, the Voice that has been talking to us. It worked." Marta exclaimed.

"Thanks to you, yes it did."

"Do you have a name?" Sam asked

"I have got so used to you calling me the Voice, that I think I shall remain as that."

"Err ok." Nikki responded. "I don't mean to offend, but are you a boy or girl, it is kind of difficult to tell?"

"I am neither and both. I am made from all of you, so I am the sum of your parts and your powers."

"Ok, we will just wait until you need to go to the toilet then." Nikki joked and Sam began to laugh. Marta darted a look at them, in the motherly manner that she had become used to, and immediately shut down their silly natures.

"So now you are here, what is next?" Marta asked.

"First we should go outside and then it will be easier to explain. Namaka if you would be kind enough to take us to the door." Voice responded.

With that Namaka managed to summon the water to transport them across the domed vault and towards the door. They then proceeded along the passageway, that they had arrived down, and to the outside. They were not quite prepared for what they saw next.

As they exited the building, they were initially blinded by the sun that shone down but as their eyes got accustomed to being outside once more, they realised that the barren wasteland that was there when they entered was no more. Instead, as far as the eye could see, was a lush and fertile land. Greenery had grown everywhere and a stream ran through it all, providing all the nourishment the land required. The group stood in amazement at the change that had happened to the landscape unable to utter a word; instead just choosing to revel in the beauty of their surroundings.

"You have done all this." Said Voice. "Your combined powers generated together have caused a chain reaction that will spread around the world allowing it to heal itself."

"So we have done it!" exclaimed Marta.

"Not quite. Whilst you have stranded Lyra, she will return stronger and better equipped to cause more damage. Until we rid the world of her powers it will be in danger. So we must get stronger ourselves and be ready when the time comes to restore the balance needed. We will need to train hard and you will need develop your powers to their full potential. Enjoy this moment for now because there is much to do. This is not the end. It is just the beginning."

S.J. Barker

The publishers and authors would like to thank Russell Spencer, Matt Vidler, Susan Woodard, Janelle Hope Leonard West, Lianne Bailey-Woodward, Laura Jayne Humphrey and Heidi Hollowbread for their work, without which this book would not have been possible.

About the Publisher

L.R. Price Publications is dedicated to publishing books by undiscovered, talented authors.

We use a mixture of traditional and modern publishing methods to bring our authors' words to the wider world.

We print, publish, distribute and market books in a variety of formats including paper and hard back, electronic books e-books, digital audio books and online.

If you are an author interested in getting your book published; or a book retailer interested in selling our books, please contact us.

www.lrpricepublications.com

L.R. Price Publications Ltd, 27 Old Gloucester Street, London, WC1N 3AX. (0203) 051 9572
publishing@lrprice.com

Printed in Great Britain
by Amazon